T0208913

SNATCHED
FROM THE FIRE

A MAN OF STAIN

DR. LOIS E. CHARLES

BALBOA.
PRESS
A DIVISION OF HAY HOUSE

Balboa Press books may be ordered through booksellers or by contacting:

Balboa Press
A Division of Hay House
1663 Liberty Drive
Bloomington, IN 47403
www.balboapress.com
1 (877) 407-4847

Print information available on the last page.

ISBN: 978-1-9822-0430-3 (sc)
ISBN: 978-1-9822-0431-0 (e)

Balboa Press rev. date: 05/22/2018

DEDICATION

This book is dedicated in the honor of my mother the late *Gussie Mae Charles*, whom after my father the late (*Elder H.K. Charles*) pasted away, tried her best to continue to steer her children in the Christian way.

AUTHOR'S NOTE

W**e** must begin by asking. Why did I write a story quoting from the scripture in the book of Jude 22-23(NKJV)? Well, it is because it is meant to *open men's eyes and minds* to the truth. There are few people who can grasp and understand abstract ideas; most people think in pictures. We could for long enough use the words, *"the transforming power of Christ,"* and at the end of it no one would be very much the wiser; but if we would say, "The transforming power of Christ is like leaven that a woman took and hid in three measures of meal, when placed in the oven, even though you don't see the leaven, it's working changing the whole character of the bread. Matt. 13:33(NKJV)," no more description is needed.

If a man wishes to teach people about things which they do not understand, he must begin from things which they do understand. The surest way to interest people is to tell them a story; truth being put in the form of a story or parable; *"an earthly story with a heavenly meaning."*

When Jesus wished to open men's minds to some of God's truth, he did it by telling them a story. Jesus used earthly things to lead men's minds to heavenly things. Paul said, *"That the visible world is designed to make known the invisible things of God (Romans 1: 20 (NKJV).* One of the greatest reasons Jesus used parables was that He wanted to tell men stories of things with which they were well acquainted, and by that they can understand better into what He was trying to teach them about truth.

This is exactly what Nathan did with David. He told him a story, it reads: *Then the Lord sent Nathan to David. And he came to him, and said to him: "There were two men in one city, one rich and the other poor. The rich man had exceedingly many flocks and herds. But the poor man had nothing, except one little ewe lamb which he had bought and nourished; and it grew up together with him and with his children. It ate of his own food and drank from his own cup and lay in his bosom; and it was like a daughter to him. And a traveler came to the rich man, who refused to take from his own flock and from his own herd to prepare one for the wayfaring man who had come to him; but he took the poor man's lamb and prepared it for the man who had come to him." Then David anger was greatly aroused against the man, and he said to Nathan, "As the Lord lives, the man who has done this shall surely die! And he shall restore fourfold for the lamb, because he did this thing and because he had no pity." Then Nathan said to David, "You are the man!"* (2nd Samuel 12: 1-7NKJV). David was to take that story and apply it to himself for what he had sinned against the Lord.

That is what Jesus was always doing in His parables. He told a story the meaning of which anyone could *see*, and the *hearers* could not help passing some kind of judgment even as the story was being told. Jesus used parables to essentially open men's minds and eyes to the truth that they had been blind and didn't understand.

If we remember the situation in which a parable was spoken will always shed a flood of light on its meaning, and that in every case Jesus is throwing into bold relief one aspect of the truth, then when we put the stories all together we shall gain an unmatched *insight* into the mind of the Master Teacher, Jesus Christ.

INTRODUCTION

This is a true story in the sense of what is happening in the lives of people as well as Christians in our society today. It is a parable of an *earthly story* with a *heavenly meaning*. The aim of this story is to bring out the examples of what happens when we drift away from obedience to God as well as our parents. It's a very high price to pay in life when our weaknesses become overwhelming to the point of disaster in our lives. Goodness lies in the choice between the higher and the lower thing.

You will see how the choices we make in life for ourselves can really determine how we live. God gives us free will to choose between life in Him and death in sin. The fact remains is that the instinct of man is that he is free to do what he likes.

You will feel the heartbeat of mothers who want the best for their children. How much we owe to the influence of godly parents, and especially godly mothers. Many great men of the past have been richly blessed by what they learned at their mother's knees.

The difference between *fate* and *destiny* is that fate is what we are compelled to do; *destiny* is what we are meant to do. We have a destiny but we are not fated. What we are meant to do as Christians is to put ourselves on God's side within the world. In which we will see in this story of how those that are compelled to do things because of the power of sin, and the destiny of those that are meant to be. You will also see the need to be strong in the faith before reclaiming the lost.

When parental advice is followed, it becomes a graceful wreath on the head and ornamental chains about the neck, which is a poetic way of saying that obedience brings honor and moral beauty to the life of a wise child.

In the book of Jude 1:22, 23(NKJV) it reads: *"Some of them you must argue out of their error while they are still wavering. Others you must rescue by snatching them out of the fire. Others you must pity and fear at the same time, hating the garment stained by the flesh."*

Some of them you must argue out of their error, while they are still wavering: You will see in this story how a fifteen year old girl who had ran away from home unknowingly about to be entrapped into slave prostitution *but was still wavering* with uncertainty and was *argued out of her error* while there was still time to save her.

There are those who have to be snatched from the fire: Sometimes in life once we start out doing the wrong things and the more we try to swim to stay on top of fiery water, the more we begin to drown. You will see how James who started out in the right way but fell into situations that he became helpless to save himself and had to be snatched from the fire of adultery, drugs and alcohol forcibly, even against his will.

There are those whom we must pity and fear at one and the same time, hating the garment stained by the flesh: In this story James is a school counselor, a minister, a husband and father, whom tried to rescue one of his troubled students, but by not being strong in the faith became overwhelmingly attracted to his students mother whom he felt pity for in the life style that she was living.

The old saying remains true; we must love the sinner but hate the sin. Before a man can rescue others, he must himself be strong in the faith. His own feet must be firm on the ground before he can throw a lifebelt to the man who is likely to be swept away.

The truth is that the rescue of those in error is not for everyone to attempt. Those who would win others for Christ must themselves be very sure of him; and those who would fight the disease of sin must themselves have the strong antiseptic of a healthy faith. Ignorance can never be met with ignorance, or even with partial knowledge. It can only be met by the affirmation, "I know whom I have believed."

AUTHOR'S PREFACE

There are parents whom have the best dreams for their children to succeed in life academically as well as spiritually. Yes a child is born and it is the most beautiful thing that you are seeing. The little wrinkles on their faces, their little hands and feet. You immediately look for traits of the father and the mother. Oh what a beautiful child that we made together!

Then comes the teenage years and you began to see the small changes in their personalities that is neither yours nor your husband's. So you began to ask yourself, "Where did she or he get this from?" With strong discipline, you try to deal with it gradually as it comes, weaning out the bad with the good. Then finally you think that you've got them back on the right road. So you thank your God and pat yourself on the back.

Then all of a sudden you hear of things that your child is doing or has done and immediately you say, "That's not by child, I didn't raise my child that way, you have to be mistaken!"

This generation is described in *Proverbs 30: 11-16(NKJV)*, where it bears a striking resemblance to the generation living today and the one which will exist in the last days. In 2 Timothy 3: 1-2(NKJV) says, *"But know this, that in the last days perilous times will come: For men will be lovers of themselves, lovers of money, boasters, proud, blasphemers, disobedient to parents, unthankful, unholy."*

Notice the following feature in *Proverbs 30:11, 17:25 (NKJV):*

Disrespectful to parents: They curse their father and show no gratitude to their mother, thus breaking the fifth Commandment (Exodus 20: 12NKJV). The hostility of children towards their parents is one of the characteristics of our decadent society. One of the great sorrows of parenthood is to have a child who causes nothing but grief and bitterness.

A child who has been disciplined properly will bring delight and rest to his parents instead of anxiety and heartache. A child who mistreats or slanders his father or mother is shameful and disgraceful himself and brings disgrace and reproach to his heartbroken parents. It is small thanks for all their parents have done for them.

Trouble is easy to get into, but hard to get out. If all of our children would think of the consequences before their actions, it can make a big difference in the outcome of many situations.

Influence plays a big role in the lives of children in our society today. Influence is very powerful whether we realize it or not, even after the parent have spent years of instilling in them truth and obedience. Yes that's how powerful *influence* is! And that's because very few of our children are brave enough to stand alone. I was taught from a young age by my father to stand up for truth and what's right even if I had to stand alone.

Often when a young man or woman ruins their lives, the explanation is given that they got in with the wrong crowd. Life is full of *enticements*. As parents you must have the courage and backbone to say "No" a thousand times a week.

In our society today it is sad to say that parents are out living their children. The elderly are living longer and young are dying faster. The young is to produce to carry on the generations, the elderly cannot. We are at a breach of a fruitless world. This should lead us on our knees in prayer and defending the faith.

We must study to be able to defend the faith and to give a reason for the hope that is in us. We must know what we believe so that we can meet error with truth; and we must make ourselves able to defend the faith in such a way that our graciousness and sincerity may win others to it.

To do this we must banish all uncertainty from our minds and all arrogance and intolerance from our approach to others.

We must be ready to speak in time. Many would have been saved from error of thought and of action, if someone else had only spoken in time. Sometimes we hesitate to speak, but there are many times when silence is cowardly and can cause more harm than speech could ever cause. One of the greatest tragedies in life is when someone comes to us and says, "I would never have been in the mess I am now in, if someone had only spoken to me."

"SNATCHED FROM THE FIRE"

This is a hot and sunny day on a Thursday about 7:00p.m. Eunice is on the bus on her way home after being discharged from the army. She's sitting next to the window looking out as she arrives in her home town. Her family is waiting at the bus station anxious to see her.

When the bus arrives at the station, Eunice gets off and gets her luggage. As she walks towards the inside of the bus station, she spots her mother (Fannie Mae Gibson), and her brother (James Gibson). Eunice yells out, "hey everybody." They turn and see that it's Eunice and they all rush towards each other hugging and kissing each other.

James says, "Girl you look like you ran everything in that place." Her Mother says, "She sure does." Eunice is hugging her mother with tears in her eyes and then hugs her brother (James). Eunice says, "Come on everybody let's go to the car and head home." James grabs Eunice's luggage and they head out to the car.

They all enter the house and her mother yells out, "She's here!" James two children John and Sharon run up to Eunice. She picks them up and kisses them. James tells Eunice, "You see my two monsters?" Eunice says, "My, look how they've grown." James's wife Brenda is in the kitchen taking the ham out of the oven. Brenda places the ham on top of the stove and hurries out of the kitchen and greets Eunice. James says, "There's my Baby." Brenda and Eunice hug and kiss each other. Brenda says, "Everybody have a seat at the table dinner is ready."

Everybody's sitting at the table and James says, "Let us bow our heads in prayer to give God thanks for this food that we are about to receive and thank him for returning Eunice back home safe from harm and danger." So everybody bows their heads as he prays. Then the food is pasted around each dipping and placing food on their plate.

His mother says, "I am so glad my Baby is home." Eunice says, "Momma I am not a baby anymore." Her mother says, "You will always be my Baby." James teases Eunice saying, "Oh, Eunice old four-eyed Horace been asking about you. He still has a crush on you." Eunice laughs and says, "Nobody want old four-eyed Horace with those big buck teeth." Everybody bursts out and laughs.

Later that night Marsha is at a friend (Glenda's) house dancing. She's very high and dancing wildly. Then she break's off and goes to the bathroom and snorts cocaine, looks in the mirror to check if there's any coke showing in her nose and says bang to herself in the mirror. She goes back in to the party and yells, "look everybody!" Then she gets center stage and does the booty drop very sexually. Everybody looks on and shouts go head, go head, go head! Then two more girls join in and challenge her.

After the party Marsha goes home and it's about 3:00am in the morning. When she gets inside her house she tries very hard not to wake her mother. So she tips to her mother's room and eases the door open and closes it. Then she takes a deep breath relieved that she made it to her room without awaking her mother (Mrs. Green). Marsha undresses and falls into bed.

The next morning Marsha turns over and looks at the clock and sees that she has over slept for work. She rushes out of bed, runs to the bathroom, jumps in the shower and starts to get dress for work as quick as she can.

When Marsha arrives at work at the insurance company her boss Mr. Philips sees her from his glass office window, waits until she gets to her desk and comes over to her and tell her he wants to see her in his office. Marsha gets up from her desk and follows him to his office. As he sits down at his desk Mr. Philips says to her, "Have a seat." Marsha sits down looking very nervous. Mr. Philips tells her that this is her second time arriving to work over an hour late, that he's not going to tolerate it much longer and that the next time she's late he will have to let her go. Marsha apologize saying to him that she missed the bus and it won't happen again. Mr. Philips says, "I should hope not. Maybe you need to get up in the mornings an hour earlier than usual to try to get to work on time." Marsha says, "Yes sir I will from now on and again I apologize for being late again." Then Marsha gets up from the chair and walks back to her desk.

Later that night James is in the den looking over some folders of the students those he councils at work. His wife Brenda is in the kid's room getting them dress for bed. Sharon the daughter says, "Mommy can I sleep with you and daddy tonight just in case I have a bad dream?" Her mother says, "No you're a big girl now you should sleep in your own bed." So Sharon says, "How about if I sleep with John?" John says, "No I don't want a girl sleeping with me." Brenda says, "Okay guys nobody is going to sleep with anybody." She picks up Sharon in her arms and says to John, "Don't forget to say your prayers, and you young lady goes with me to your room." She takes Sharon to her room and lays her in bed, pulls the cover over her and says, "Close your eyes, now repeat after me. Now I lay me down to sleep and pray to my Lord my soul he'll keep. If I should die before I wake, I pray Lord my soul you'll take, Amen." Brenda gives her a kiss, turns the light off leaving the little night light on and leaves the room.

Then Brenda goes where James is in the den sneaks up to him and began kissing him on his ear and wants to snuggle. James smiles while still trying to concentrate on his lesson plan. He tells her, "Wait a minute Baby I am just about finished." But she continues kissing him on the neck and then on his lips. James can't resist and turns to her and picks her up in his arms and takes her to their room, lays her on the bed, takes his robe off and they began to make love.

Later that night Marsha is at the club with her friend Floyd. There're up on the dance floor dancing. When the music stops they return to their table. Floyd says, "Girl that was a blast! Oh we need more drinks." Marsha says, "Go order some more while I use the restroom." Floyd asks her, "More beer right?" Marsha replies, "Yes the same thing." So Floyd goes up to the bar and orders two beers while Marsha goes to the restroom. When Marsha enters the restroom, she goes into one of the stalls, sits on the toilet, opens her purse, takes out a folded dollar bill where she has her cocaine and with her small finger nail she fills the cocaine and snorts.

Floyd is at the table waiting for her impatiently wandering what's taking her so long. Finally Marsha comes out of the restroom with a big smile on her face, sits down at the table and says, "Floyd boy I am feeling no pain." Floyd laughs and says, "I know what that's about." Then Floyd pours her up the beer. Floyd begins to sip his beer and looks up and notices that Marsha is gulping her beer down real fast. Floyd says, "Marsha my goodness slow down or you won't be on your feet very long." Marsha replies, "Come on Floyd let's dance." She grabs him by the hand and they proceed to the dance floor. Marsha begins to dance very wildly and almost looses her balance. She straightens up and gets back on course. Floyd is just dancing and having a good time.

Later Marsha gets home late. Her mother (Mrs. Green) hears her come in and gets out of bed. Marsha tries to walk as quietly as she can. She doesn't know that her mother is standing at her bedroom door waiting for her. When Marsha thinks she has a clear shot, her mother confronts her. Marsha is too high to even stand up straight. Mrs. Green says with a worried look on her face, "Marsha you look a mess like you've been drinking. You think I don't know you've been coming home late? Well I have you know I do." Marsha covers her face with her hands and says, "Momma I am sorry, but not now please. I just need to lie down. Please momma let me pass." Mrs. Green says, "I'll let you pass but we need to talk." Mrs. Green moves out of the way and Marsha straightens up a little bit. Mrs. Green looks disgusted at her as she opens the door and goes in her room. Marsha goes straight to her bed and crashes.

The next morning Marsha gets to work late again. Her boss, Mr. Phillips sees her and makes a gesture for her to come to his office. Marsha put her purse down on her desk and walks to his office. Mr. Phillips says to her, "Have a seat." Marsha sits down slowly as though she knows what he's going to say to her. Mr. Phillips says, "Marsha I am sorry to say that I will have to terminate your employment with us as of today. You know that I've spoken to you twice before even though I knew you were late several times earlier. I was trying to give you the benefit of the doubt because you are a good employee. But after the two warnings now I am sorry, I have to let you go. Good luck on your new job search." Marsha sadly gets up from her chair and walks out of his office. She stops and grabs her purse. With her head down she quietly walks out of the office. Her coworkers look on very sadly as though they knew what had happened.

Marsha hits the streets and waits for a bus about five minutes. She notices that there is a liquor store down the street. There are cars stopped at the red light. So she walks in between them to cross to the other side. When she gets to the liquor store, she walks in and orders a pint of Gin. The store clerk reaches back and gets the pint of Gin and places it on the counter and asks her, "Would you like a chaser with that?" Marsha replies, "No that will be all." So the store clerk rings up her bill and Marsha pays him. The store clerk places the Gin in a bag and says, "Thank you." Marsha doesn't say anything she just grabs the bag and walks out of the store.

Marsha disregards catching the bus and looks for a spot so she can drink her Gin. As she walks tears begin to run down her cheeks because she began to think again about her losing her job. She keeps hearing her boss voice, "I have to let you go" over and over again. She starts to run and she notices a park near by. She finds a private bench behind some hedges and sits down, put her purse down and hurriedly folds the bag down and opens the Gin. She takes one long sip of the Gin and then another and another. She begins to cry.

Eunice is at the unemployment office filling out a job application. She's just about finished and she takes it up to the counter to the intake clerk. The clerk looks it over and tells Eunice that she will be contacted once the supervisor approves her application. Eunice says, "Thank you" and leaves.

Later at evening time Marsha arrives home. Her mother is in the kitchen cooking dinner. Her sister (Kathy) is in the living room watching television. Marsha is a little tipsy and tries to compose herself to speak to Kathy. Kathy says, "Hey Sis what's up?" Marsha tries to straighten up as much as she can and says, "You." Kathy says, "You look like you've been through a storm." Marsha laughs it off and heads straight to her bedroom trying to avoid her mother (Mrs. Green). Mrs. Green comes out of the kitchen just missing Marsha about a minute. She looks at Kathy with a question mark on her face asking, "Was that Marsha I heard you talking to?" Kathy says, "Yes Momma that was Marsha." Mrs. Green says, "I thought I heard you talking to somebody. Dinner is about ready. Are you all going to bible study tonight?" Kathy says, "I am going but I don't know about Marsha, she doesn't look like she's feeling too good." Mrs. Green asks, "What makes you think that she's not feeling good?" Kathy says, "She looks terrible and acting kind of funny." Mrs. Green says, "Well I'll check on her later, I better get back in this kitchen before my biscuits burn."

The next day Marsha dresses as though she is going to work because she doesn't want her mother to know that she lost her job. She gets her big purse so she can put her changing clothes and shoes in to walk the beat.

Marsha catches the bus across town and gets off where she sees the prostitutes hang out. She goes into one of the fast food restaurant's bathroom to change clothes. She comes out looking totally different with heavy makeup on, hot shorts, very high heel shoes and low cut blouse. The man at the register looked puzzled as though he's wondering if she was the same person that went in the bathroom. So he glanced a little at the door of the ladies restroom as though he is expecting someone else to come out.

Marsha walks over where she sees the prostitutes hanging out. There were two lady prostitutes and one drag queen. The drag queen (Gucci) spots her and says to the other ladies, "Now who is this walking up here? I just know she's not coming over here, this is our block. Somebody please tell me she's not headed this way." The other two ladies started laughing at what Gucci was saying and steady looking at Marsha as she is steadily walking towards them. Marsha sees the look on their faces and knows that they are wondering where she's going and where she came from. So she picks up her game a little bit and tries to act brave as though she knows the streets.

When Marsha got a little closer she began to smile and says, "Hey girls, what going on?" Gucci was the first to speak and says, "Who you might be?" Marsha tells them her name. As the other two ladies looks on, Gucci says, "You must be on your way to some other place because I know it's not here." Marsha says, "Well, I saw you all over here and I decided to join you." Gucci says in a joking way, "So little miss red riding hood you just bought your little tootsie over here and thought you can just hook up with us just like that?" One of the other ladies (Snow White) says, "Gucci now don't be so hard on her now, you know how you were when you tried to join up with us. Sugar what your name?" Marsha tells them her name. Snow White says, "My name is Snow White." Gucci interrupts and says, "Can't you tell?" Everybody laughs because Snow White is black as they come. Snow White says, "Before I was so rudely interrupted, my name is Snow White, this is Peaches and the rude one is Gucci. So you want to join up with us?" Marsha says, "Yes if you all don't mine." Gucci says, "Girl you better act stronger than that because it gets ruff out here sometimes, you better act like you know up in here. Look at my strut." Gucci walks the beat twisting and placing his hand on his hips and puts the scarf around his neck and holds it in front with two hands and twist harder. Marsha walks behind him trying to copy him and Snow White and Peaches looks on and sings, "Go head, go head, go head."

A man pulls over and toots his horn. Gucci turns around and walks up to his car, sticks his head in the car window on the passenger side and says to the man, "It's now or never." The man says, "I want that one there." He was referring to Marsha. So

Gucci tells Marsha that the man wants her. Marsha was shocked that she got a date so fast. So she walks up to the car and gets in and they drive away. Gucci turns to Snow White and Peaches and says, "I know I didn't see what just happen. This got to be a bad dream. Wake me up somebody." Snow White and Peaches start laughing.

While riding, the man ask Marsha what's her name. Marsha tells him her name. He says, "My name is Frank. You're new around here right?" Marsha lies and says, "I am new on this block but not new to the business. Bye the way, where are we going?" Frank says, "I know a little spot called Momma's House. It's not too far from here. You look a little nervous, you want to stop and pick up a drink or something?" Marsha says, "Yes I wouldn't mine if we do?" Frank says, "How about a little Hennessy?" Marsha says, "Sounds good to me." Frank spots a liquor store and pulls over. He gets out of the car and goes in the liquor store to buy the Hennessey. While Frank is in the liquor store Marsha opens her purse and pulls out a folded dollar bill. She opens it and uses her longest finger nail to snort the coke. She tries to hurry and finish snorting before Frank get back.

Frank returns to the car, gets in and hands Marsha the bag with the drink in it. Frank says to Marsha, "Well we are all set. Now we're on our way to Big Momma's House." Marsha just looks at him and smiles.

They enter the door at Big Momma's House. Sitting behind the counter is Big Momma with her loud red wig, heavy makeup, and extra long eyelashes. She looks like an oversize baby doll. Frank says, "Hey Momma, what room you have for me today? You know my lucky number." Big Momma laughs and says, "Sugar you know Big Momma's going to fix you up, go to room five." Frank says, "Alright Big Momma" and He and Marsha begins to walk away. Big Momma says, "Hey Sugar now you know the rooms are not free." Frank turns around and says, "Oh, my bag, now Big Momma you know I believe in paying." Frank hands Big Momma a twenty dollar bill and tells her to keep the change. Big Momma says, "Sugar you know I will." They both laugh.

Frank opens the door for Marsha and they both go in the room. Marsha goes and sits at the little table, puts her purse down and the bag with the Hennessey in it. She takes the cups out and began to pour up the drinks. Frank is taking his clothes off down to his underwear. Marsha starts to sip on her drink. Frank comes over and sits at the table with her. Marsha tells him that she likes to be paid up front. Frank asks Marsha how much does she charge. Marsha tells him two-hundred dollars. Frank says, "No problem I just hope you're worth it." Frank gets his wallet out of his pants pocket and counts two-hundred dollars out and hands it to her. Marsha takes the money and puts it in her purse. Frank then sits down at the table with Marsha and they both drink for about twenty minutes. Frank gets up and takes Marsha by the hand. Marsha gets up and starts to take her clothes off. Frank goes and gets in bed. When Marsha finishes undressing, she joins Frank in bed. Marsha starts to look very sexy at Frank and they lay together. Marsha just lays there motionless with her eyes closed.

It's about noon time same day, Eunice is on the phone talking to the director of correction. She tells her that she was chosen for the position as a correctional officer for women at the Women's Correctional Center. Eunice says, "Thank you." The director asks Eunice if she had a pen or pencil handy. She gives her the address to the facility and the day she's to start. Then the director tells her she'll see her then. Eunice tells her thank you, hangs up the phone and jumps for joy. Eunice rushes to the kitchen where her mom is and tells her the good news. Her mother says, "Oh that's wonderful! When do you start?" Eunice says, "Monday." They both hug each other. Eunice spends around with great joy. Her mother looks on very happy for her.

Eunice sniffs a little bit and says, "Momma that doesn't smell like lunch." Her mother says, "No it's not lunch but you can have some for lunch." I am cooking dinner early because I want take some over to your crazy uncle Melvin. You can make yourself a meatloaf sandwich for lunch if you want to; it's over there on the counter top." Eunice says, "Okay momma." So Eunice gets the bread from off the top of the refrigerator and makes her a sandwich, grabs her soda from the refrigerator, and goes and sits down in the living room. She places the soda and sandwich on the table in front of the sofa, turns on the television and began to eat her sandwich.

The same day, Gucci and Marsha are walking the beat. Two men pull over along side of them. The man on the passenger side says, "Ladies, what's up?" Gucci stops and turns around and says, "I am what's up." Then his friend in the driver's seat says, "Ask her about the other one, I like her." So his friend says, "Why don't you and your friend get in." Gucci turns around to Marsha and says, "Come on girl he's talking about you too." So they both get in the back seat.

While on the road, Gucci says, "I am Gucci and this is Marsha." The two men introduce themselves. Gucci asks, "So where are we off to?" The man in the passenger seat asks, "Where do you all do your tricks?" Gucci says, "At Big Momma's house, just keep driving until you get at the second red light and make a right." Then Gucci pull out a pint of Vodka and he and Marsha take turns drinking it straight out of the bottle. Gucci says, "Fellows have some?" They both say, "No thanks we're straight." Gucci takes a big sip and starts to sing in a real flat voice, "Touch me in the morning and then just walk away." Marsha starts laughing.

Mrs. Gibson, (Eunice's mother) arrives at her brother's house (Melvin), with some food wrapped up for his dinner. She spots Melvin walking in the yard with dark shades on and a blind man cane in his hand as though he was really blind. As she walks up to him she says, "Melvin what happened to you?" Melvin sees her and rushes to his front door not saying a word or even looking at her. She keeps calling him, "Melvin, Melvin what happened?" Melvin makes it inside and hides behind the door. As soon as Mrs. Gibson comes in the house, he quickly shuts the door behind her. She looks at him and asks him again, "Melvin what happened to you, you can't see?" Melvin takes the sunglasses off and puts his cane down. He looks at her and says, "You almost blew my cover! You know how nosy these neighbors are." Mrs. Gibson falls out laughing and says, "Melvin you are just as crazy as you can be. What are you up to now?" Melvin says, "You know I applied for disability." As Mrs. Gibson places the food on the table she says, "You are a nut is what you are. I brought you some dinner over and to see how you're doing. I should have known you would be up to something." They both laughed.

Later that evening Marsha gets home dressed as though she's been to work. Her sister and mother haven't arrived home yet. So Marsha notices that they're not there and rushes to her room. Marsha throws her purse on the bed, undresses and takes a shower. Then she dresses and goes to the kitchen and fixes herself a plate of food that her mother had cooked earlier. She goes to her room and turns on the television, sits on the bed and eats her dinner.

The phone rings. Marsha picks up the phone. It's Eunice calling her. Eunice says, "Hey Tee." Marsha knows its Eunice because she's the only one that calls her by that name. So Marsha screams, "Eunice you got to be home!" Eunice says, "You know it girl. We've got to get together and talk about things; you know what I am talking about." Marsha says, "I know that's right girl." Eunice says, "How about I pick you up tomorrow night and we go out? You just name the place it's my treat." Marsha says, "Okay Tee I know just the place. What time are you coming?" Eunice says, "About seven o'clock." Marsha says, "I'll be ready." Eunice says, "Okay Tee, I'll see you then bye."

Marsha hears her mother coming in the front door and rushes to the living room to tell her Mom (Mrs. Green). Marsha says, "Momma quest who just called me?" Her mom asks, "Who?" Marsha says, "Eunice, she's back from the army." Mrs. Green says, "That's wonderful. Is she coming over?" Marsha says, "She's coming over tomorrow to pick me up we're going out." Mrs. Green says, "I know you're going to be excited to see her." Marsha says, "Yea momma I can't wait! Momma you know the Army was the only thing that separated us. We were always together people thought that we were sisters." Mrs. Green says, "Yes you girls grew up together. I felt like she was my own daughter. You all are about the same age too aren't you?" Marsha says, "Yea momma she's twenty-one and so am I." Mrs. Green says, "I know you two are going to have a lot to talk about." Marsha says, "Yea momma you know I've got to bring her up to date on everything." Mrs. Green just smiles at Marsha.

It's Saturday night and Eunice is at the door ringing the door bell at Marsha's house. Marsha's mother opens the door. Mrs. Green says, "Eunice is that you? My, my, my, come on in." Eunice hugs Mrs. Green. Mrs. Green looks Eunice over and says, "You have grown into a wonderful young lady." Eunice says, "Thank you Mrs. Green." Mrs. Green says, "Come on and have a seat, Marsha should be out soon." Eunice sits down on the sofa. Marsha comes out and spots Eunice sitting on the sofa. Marsha says, "Eunice is that really you?!" Eunice gets up and they both hug each other. Marsha says, "Momma we're leaving." Mrs. Green yells from the kitchen, Okay baby you all be safe." Marsha says as they head for the door, "We will momma." Eunice says, "Bye Mrs. Green."

It's Sunday and Eunice and her mother (Mrs. Gibson) are sitting in the congregation. Also Marsha, her mother (Mrs. Green), and her sister (Kathy) are also in the congregation. The Choir is singing. James and Pastor Williams are sitting in the pulpit listening at the Choir singing. After the Choir finishes singing, Pastor Williams gets up and walks to the podium and says, "Let everybody say amen." The congregation says, "Amen." Pastor Williams says, "We give honor to the Lord and Savior Jesus Christ, to our Elders and Ministers of the Gospel, to our Deacons, our Mothers and to the congregation. It is a privilege and an honor to be able to stand before you today. I thank God for our lovely Choir for singing those lovely songs of Zion. They really touched my heart. If it wasn't for the Lord on my side, I don't know where I would be right now. I could have been sleeping in my grave, but God saw it fit for me to yet be here.

Now we're not going to prolong the time. I would like to introduce to you the speaker of the hour. He is a young man whom I have known since he was a little boy. Yes he grew up right here in this Church. He's a father and a husband. He attended College at West Virginia State where he obtained his degree in Education and Counseling. After graduation the Lord called him into the Ministry. He's a man with a big heart and concern for others. So now I would like to present to you none other than Minister James Gibson."

James gets up from his seat with his Bible in his hand, walks up to the podium and shakes Pastor William's hand, places his Bible on the podium and says, "I thank my Lord and Savior Jesus Christ for being in your midst today. I would like to give honor to my Pastor Elder Williams and to the entire congregation."

Eunice and her mother proudly look on. James announced the title of his text and began to preach.

Later that day James, his wife and kids are at his mother's house for dinner. They're all sitting at the table eating. His mother commends James on the sermon he preached at Church that day. His mother says, "James I was so proud of you in the service today. That sermon really touched my heart. You know that's true, sometimes we do forget how much God has done for us." James smiles and says, "Yea momma we sometimes need to be reminded of that. We get caught up in our daily occupations and always wanting this and that until we don't even give thanks or realize what God have already done for us." His mother says, "You are so right." Eunice says, "Momma don't get him started he'll be preaching all over again." Everybody laughs and continue eating.

It's Monday morning and Eunice is at her new job. She's in the office with Ms. Stone the Director of Corrections. Ms. Stone explains to her what her duties are as a Correctional Officer. Then Ms. Stone introduces Eunice to Ms. White her supervisor and co-workers. Ms. White tells Eunice that she's welcomed aboard. Eunice replies, "Thank you, I am happy to be a part of the team." Ms. White says, "Now follow me while I show you where the inmates are." Eunice follows her.

Marsha is on the beat with Gucci. Gucci says to Marsha, "Girl lets pick it up a bit. You better act like you know out here. Look girl I think I see one slowing up." Gucci stops and bends over like he dropped something on the ground. The man in the car notices and pulls over. Gucci spreads his legs and looks at the man from between his legs. The man toots his horn and Gucci stands up, shakes his butt, turns around and says, "Bam!" Marsha starts laughing and says, "Girl you so crazy." Gucci gets in the car with the man and says to Marsha, "See you on the rebound."

James is at the school in his office counseling a student. The student is ten years old and his name is Edward Spencer. James says, "So Edward what seems to be your problem this morning with your teacher Ms. Clark?" Edward holds his head down and refuses to talk. James says, "Edward are you hearing me?" Edward just shakes his head but still refuse to answer. James says, "Well in my notes here it says that you seem irritated with Ms. Clark and that you don't want to participate in some of the activities that she has for the class to do and that you constantly fall asleep in class. Is that true Edward?" Edward continues to hold his head down not saying a word. James says, "Edward I am here to help you and the only way that I can do that is for you to tell me what seems to be the problem. I won't get angry at you or scorn you, I am your friend. You can tell me anything." Edward looks up at James with a solemn face. James says, "Don't worry we're going to work this out together. Now give me a few minutes to look over at your file again." James has Edward's file in front of him and he opens it up. James begins to review the file and notices that Edward is an only child and his mother is a single parent.

So James says, "Edward I see in your file that it's just you and your mother living in the home. Do you know where your father lives?" Edward answers, "No." James asks, "When was the last time you've seen your father?" Edward answers, "I've never seen my father before." Now that James has gotten some response from Edward, he asks Edward, "Edward what seems to be the problem that you don't want to participate and falling asleep in class? Your teacher says that you are rude to her and you pick on the kids in class. Do you like coming to school?" Edward drops his head again and says, "No." James asks, "Now why is that?" Edward doesn't answer.

James says, "Edward do you hear me talking to you?" Edward nods his head for yes. James says, "Edward stop nodding your head, talk to me." Edward looks up and says, "Because I am tired and sleepy." James asks, "Are you having problems sleeping at night?" Edward sadly says, "Yes." James asks, "What seems to be the problem that's causing you not to be able to sleep at night?" Edward says, "I have to sit on the steps late at night until momma quests leaves." James looks at Edward puzzled. James asks, "Why do you have to sit outside can't you go to your room?" Edward says, "We don't have any rooms, just a living room and a bathroom." James sadly says, "Oh I understand. What kind of work does your mother do?" Edward says, "She doesn't have a job." James says, "Well maybe I can try and help her find a job, how about that?" Edward just smiles.

James says, "Edward I am going to send you back to class. Like I said, I am here for you and we are going to work things out together for the better. Do you think you can behave yourself until then?" Edward says, "Yes Sir." James says, "That's what I want to hear. I'll be talking with your teacher to let her know to expect some positive changes in you. My door is always open to you Edward, I am here for you. Now you go back to class and keep that chin up."

Edward gets up from his chair and says, "Thank you Sir." James gets up from his desk and opens the door for Edward to leave. Then James sits back at his desk and began to write down some notes in his files.

Later Marsha's mother (Mrs. Green) is at home dusting off the furnisher in the living room. Suddenly she remembers that she has a meeting at her church with the Home Mission Department that evening and she may not be home when Kathy and Marsha gets home. So she stops dusting and goes to end tables where the phone is and looks in her phone tablet for the girls work phone numbers. She calls Marsha's job first.

One of the insurance clerks answers the phone. Mrs. Green asks to speak to Marsha. The clerk tells her that Marsha no longer works there. Mrs. Green said, "You must be mistaken, my daughter has been working there for two years now." The clerk said, "I know but Marsha hasn't been working here for about three weeks now." Mrs. Green in shock says, "Her last name is Green, Marsha Green." The clerk says, "Yes I know she's the one I am referring to, Marsha Green." Mrs. Green hesitates for a while and then hangs up the phone. Mrs. Green flaps down on the sofa and looks worried and confused.

Later that day, Marsha is at Gucci's apartment in his bedroom changing back in her regular clothes before going home. When she comes out of the bedroom Gucci has also changed out of his drag queen clothes and has taken all his makeup off looking like a regular guy. He looks handsome and Marsha looks at him thinking that he's a friend of Gucci because this is the first time she has seen him out of drag. Marsha says, "Hello my name is Marsha." Gucci bursts out laughing and says, "Marsha you so crazy, this me Gucci!" Marsha grabs her face in amazement and says, "Gucci I thought that you were a room mate." Gucci says, "No love no one stays here but me."

Come on over here and sit down on the couch while I set up the table with the goodies." Gucci has a bar near his living room. So he walks over to his bar and gets a bottle of rum and some glasses and places them on the glass table in front of Marsha. Then he walks back to the bar to gets the cocaine from under the bar shelf that's in a fancy container and some straws for them to snort. Gucci place everything on the glass table and sits on the couch next to Marsha. Then he jumps back up and says, "Oh girl I forgot the ice." So Gucci grabs the ice container off the bar and goes to the kitchen to get some ice cubes out of the refrigerator. Gucci comes out of the kitchen with the ice cubes then stops, poses and says to Marsha, "Yippy-do-da-day, girl let's get this party started right now." Marsha laughs and says, "Sounds good to me."

Gucci places everything on the table and sits down on the sofa by Marsha. Then he puts ice cubes in Marsha's glass and his glass, pours the rum in the glasses while Marsha gets the blade and makes the lines on the glass table with the cocaine. Each one gets a straw and starts to snort. Then Gucci looks at Marsha as a man looks at women. Marsha looks at Gucci and says, "Oh no you're not, you look like you want to kiss me." Gucci gets closer to Marsha and says, "Why not, after all I am a man."

Marsha stands up and says, "Hold on I thought you like men." Gucci says, "Oh that's just a front to do what I do." Gucci stands up and puts his hands on Marsha's cheeks and says, "I am attracted to you and all I can say is this moment feels good with you." Then he kisses her. Marsha pulls back as he kisses her and laughs and says, "Gucci you need get somewhere and sit down, you so crazy." Gucci looking yet very serious pulls her up to him and kisses her deeply. Marsha pulls away gently and looks at Gucci in a confusing way and says, "I better be going" and turns around to get her purse. Gucci gently grabs her by her hand but Marsha takes her hand away, gets her purse and says as she walks towards the door, "Good night Gucci I enjoyed myself, thanks for everything." Gucci with a stunned look on his face walks behind her as she opens the door and leaves.

Marsha gets home and only her sister (Kathy) is home. Kathy is in her room polishing her nails with the door open. On the way to her room Marsha stops at Kathy's room door and says, "I am home, where's Mom?" Kathy says, "Mom is at the church, didn't she call you at your job?" Marsha turns around not saying a word and heads for her room. Marsha throws her purse down on the bed and lies across the bed wondering if her mother called her job or not. Then she sits up on the bed, places her hands over her face and says, "Oh no."

Mrs. Green is at the Church in her Home Mission meeting. The meeting is over and Mrs. Green is shaking every ones hands as she proceeds out of the door. It's about 8:00 pm as Mrs. Green drives home.

The same night James is at his student's house that he counseled at school. It's a rooming house. James finds a place to park and goes to the door and knocks. James notices Edward sitting on the steps. James says, "Hey Edward." Edward looks up smiles and says, "Hi Mr. Gibson" and dropped his head. James looks at him knowing that something is wrong and asks, "Is your mother home?" Edwards says with his head still down, "Yes she's home." James says, "Thanks." Then he knocks on the door. Edward's mother (Ms. Betty Spencer) is in bed with one of her clients. She hears the knock on the door and says to the man, "Charlie, hold on a minute let me see who's at the door." Charlie pulls her back and says "Come on baby I am loosing my time." James knocks again and Ms. Spencer tells Charlie, No Charlie let me up to see who's knocking my son is out there something could be wrong." Charlie says, "Okay" and lets her up.

She cracks the door and sees James and says, "Yes can I help you?" James says, "Yes my name is Mr. Gibson. I am your son Edward's counselor at his school and I stopped by to talk to you about some concerns we have regarding your son's behavior." Ms. Spencer tells James to give her a few minutes and closes the door. She turns around and tells Charlie, "Get up and get dressed!" Charlie jumps out of bed and says, "Who is it, what's wrong!" Ms. Spencer says, "Just hurry and get dressed!" Charlie rushes to get dressed. Ms. Spencer rushes to get dressed herself and says, "Hurry Charlie, hurry!" Charlie says, "I am going as fast as I can!" Ms. Spencer straightens the top spread on the bed and sprays some room deodorant and says to Charlie, "Go, go!" Charlie rushing to the door says, "I am going!" Charlie opens the door not looking back and rushes down the stairs. James looks on wondering what's wrong with him being in such a hurry.

Then Ms. Spencer opens the door and invites James in. James goes in and Ms. Spenser grabs a chair from the lamp stand for James to sit down while she sits on the bottom edge of the bed. James notices that the place was very small. It had no kitchen just a room with a microwave on a table and small refrigerator, a bathroom, closet, and dresser. He looks at Ms. Spencer and she has just a robe on. She has heavy makeup on, long eyelashes, and a long brunette wig on her head. James quickly notices that she's very attractive and sexy looking. Ms. Spencer smiles and says, "You were saying something about my son's behavior in school?" James staring at her says, "Yes, first of all let me formally introduce myself. My name is Mr. James Gibson and I am a Counselor at your son's school." Ms. Spencer says, "I am Edwards mother Ms. Betty Spencer but you can call me Betty and nice meeting you." James smiles and says, "Likewise, Ms. Spencer Edward was sent to me by his teacher for counseling and in talking to Edward some things that he said kind of puzzled me that caused some concerns and that's why I am here. Ms. Spencer Edward claims that he goes to bed late because he has to sit outside while you entertain clients.

Now I wasn't born yesterday Ms. Spencer I have an idea of what he's talking about. Don't get me wrong, I am not here to judge what your life styles are, I do believe that there's a reason for everything. We may not agree with some of the choices that are made but yet I respect you as an individual. God gives us free will he offers us a choice to choose Him and even those who sometimes don't. Yet he still loves us and blesses us giving us time because He's not willing that any should perish." Ms. Spencer says, "You sound like a preacher." James smiles and says, "I am a Minister at my church. In other words I am studying to be a Pastor one day.

Ms. Spencer if you don't mine me asking, what is the highest grade level that you've earned?" Ms. Spencer says, "I have a degree in computer graphics believe it or not." James says, "Excuse me for asking but did you ever pursue your career in that area of study?" Ms. Spencer says, "What you mean is what happened. To make a long story short I got strung out on drugs and hit rock bottom." James says, "Well Ms. Spencer I am going to try and help you on my own time and see if we can work something out to make things a little better for you in the interest of your son, because the rate that you are going you are going to loose him and he's going to loose a mother.

Now I know you don't want that to happen. But in the mean time to keep things in perspective so that you won't loose your son, you are going to have to make sure that you make arrangements so that he gets his proper rest and nutrition to be able to function properly in school. I know that it's none of my business the type of lifestyle you have but I won't take any excuses for how it's affecting your son. I'll be working with you and checking on you to see if there's any progress in this situation. If you sincerely want my help, I'll take out some of my free time to see what I can do. Okay Ms. Spencer? Now I am going to be leaving and thank you for your time." James shakes Ms. Spencer's hand as he gets up out of his chair. As they walk toward the door Ms. Spencer says, "I promise you that things are going to change from now on you'll see. I don't want to lose my son." She opens the door for James and says, "Thank you for coming good night." James says, "Good night." She leaves the door open and calls Edward to come inside. James looks on and smiles at Edward as he's leaving. (*Others you must pity and fear at the same time.*)

Mrs. Green has arrived home. She enters the front door. Kathy is in her usual place on the sofa watching television. Kathy says, "Hi Mom how was the meeting?" Mrs. Green says, "It went very well (as she places her purse on the table). Kathy asks, "What did you all discuss?" Mrs. Green says, "Oh we were talking about soul winning. Where's Marsha?" Kathy says, "In her room." Mrs. Green goes and knocks on Marsha's room door. Marsha is sitting at her dresser mirror snorting coke. She hears the knock on the door. Marsha hurries to put the coke away in the dresser draw. She looks in the mirror to check her nose to make sure no coke is visible and answers the door. Marsha opens the door and says, "Hi Mom." Mrs. Green says, "Marsha, we need to talk." Marsha leaves the door open and sits on the bed. Mrs. Green sits by her on the bed.

Mrs. Green says, "I called your job this morning, now what is going on?" Where have you been going every morning?" Marsha says very angrily, "Momma that's my business and that's all I want to say about that!" Mrs. Green says, "Don't you speak to me in that tone of voice! I am your Mother and I demand more respect than that!" The coke that Marsha had snorted begins to settle in her brain and Marsha slowly says, "Momma, not now please." Mrs. Green looks carefully at Marsha as though she suspect that Marsha is on something. Then Mrs. Green says, "What ever that is you are doing, I am not going to have it in my house."

Then Mrs. Green gets up and walks out of the door. Marsha shuts the door, turns her back to the door and slides down against the door to the floor crying because she knows her mother is catching up with her.

The same night at Big Momma's House a couple is in one of the rooms. The man is dressing and the lady is sitting on the bed watching him getting dressed. When he finishes dressing he reaches in his pocket and throws a hundred dollar bill on the bed and says, "See you around." The lady just picks up the money off the bed and the man leaves out leaving the door wide open. The lady looks on the lamp table and sees he left the bottle of Rum. She scoops over and pours herself a drink.

Big Momma notices that the lady hasn't come out of the room. So she goes to the room, peeps in and sees the lady is just sitting there on the bed weeping. Big Momma knocks a little bit because she didn't just want to walk in. The lady looks up and sees Big Momma still weeping. Big Momma walks up to her and says, "Baby what's wrong, are you alright?" The lady says, "I was thinking about my life. I make over two hundred dollars a day selling my body and it's all spent on drugs. I sleep in an abandoned house on the floor, I beg for food rather than to spend a dime on food saving it for drugs." Then she looks up at Big Momma and burst out in tears and says, "What kind of life is that? I've been on the streets since I was fourteen, I am just twenty five years old and I am tired." (*The choices we make in life really determine how we live.*)

Big Momma sits down on the bed next to her and places her arms around her and says, "Baby I only rent rooms but I know that there's a God and I believe that through His mercy, and righteousness, not ours, that if we call on him He will be there for us." Wiping her tears she looks at Big Momma and says, "I am too ashamed to go before the Lord." Big Momma says, "Mary Madeline went to him and she was a woman of many sins, they say she was a prostitute and Jesus forgave her of her sins. Jesus loved Mary and she followed Him all the way to the cross." The lady stood up and reached out her hands towards

Big Momma. Big Momma got up and they both hugged each other. The lady said, "Thank you so much, I needed that."

The next morning Marsha is up packing her things. Her mother is in the kitchen preparing breakfast. Marsha calls a cab on her cell phone. Kathy is in the kitchen with her mother getting some orange juice out of the refrigerator. Kathy takes the orange juice to the table and pours her mother some in her glass and sits down in front of her plate and pours herself some orange juice and begins to eat breakfast.

The cab pulls up in front of their house. Marsha spots the cab from her bedroom window. She grabs her luggage and rushes out of the house and gets into the cab and they drive away. Kathy says to her mother, "I guess Marsha is going to pass on breakfast this morning." Mrs. Green says, "She's probably in there pouting from our little discussion last night." Kathy says, "Did I miss out on something? What has she done now Momma?" Mrs. Green says, "Hurry up and finish your breakfast so you won't be late for work." Kathy (with a question mark on her face) says, "I heard that."

The cab pulls up to a motel. Marsha pays the cab driver, gets her luggage out of the cab and checks in to the motel.

Back at the house Kathy has left for work and Mrs. Green is finishing cleaning up the kitchen and decides to go to Marsha's room. When she gets there she knocks on the door and calls for Marsha. After not receiving an answer she turns the door knob and slowly opens the door to see what Marsha was doing. After not seeing Marsha no where in the room, she panics and began to look around checking her closet and dresser draws, she notice that everything was gone. She grabs her chest in disbelief and sits on Marsha's bed to catch her breath. She begins to cry saying, "My baby is gone. My baby is gone."

James is at his job in his office counseling a sarcastic nerd name Harold. He's in the fifth grade. He wears these thick eye glasses that makes his eyes look ten times as big. If you look at him you would think that he won't harm a fly. But this kid is smart, but by no means as innocent as he looks. Harold intimidates his teacher (Mrs. Mooney) as well as his classmates. This is why he was sent to James for counseling.

After James introduces himself, he began to tell Harold why he was sent to his office. James says, "Mrs. Mooney is displeased ...." Harold interrupts and says, "With me in class" before James could say anymore. James waited until Harold finished interrupting and began to say something else, Harold would always interrupt finishing the sentence. So finally James said, "You think you know it all, well what about this, I am going to call your parents this evening and......Harold don't you know what I am about to say next?" Harold eyes got so big through those thick glasses of his and he froze.

Later that day Marsha is at Gucci's apartment and Gucci is in his bedroom dressed in drag sitting at the mirror dresser applying his makeup getting ready to go out on the beat. Marsha is sitting in the living room lining some coke on the table in front of the sofa. She began to snort one line at a time and sips on her drink. Then Gucci comes out of his room and joins Marsha on the couch. Gucci says to Marsha, "Girl slow down or you're not going to make it out on the beat." Marsha says, "Oh yes I will. I am just trying to relieve some pressure." Gucci looks at her and says,

"What pressure?" Marsha says, "My Mom and I had a little run in. She started following up on me too close and I had to leave." Gucci says, "You mean you moved out?" Marsha says, "Yes, I didn't have much choice. Either I stay and we keep getting into arguments, or leave. I didn't want to stay there disrespecting her I love my mom. It's me not her. I just can't get it out of my mind with what she always taught us that God gives us free will and the choices we make is up to us. You see Gucci it bad when you know better, sometimes it's hard to look at myself." Gucci says, "Oh my goodness girl now you going too deep. You are going to blow my high, your high and both of us are going to miss going out on the beat. But girl I understand, now get yourself together."

Gucci asks, "Where did you move to?" Marsha says, "I checked into a motel for the time being until I find a place of my own." Gucci says, "You can stay here with me I have plenty of room here. You know I have two bedrooms here and it's enough space that we won't get in each other's way. Besides, I like you. Every since we met we've been kicking it." Marsha says, "Yea isn't that something we hit is off right away. You have a nice fancy apartment, I love it." Gucci says (as he pops his fingers), "Not only am I living like a queen, I am the queen. Welcome to my palace." They both start laughing. Marsha says, "I don't want to intrude." Gucci says, "Oh girl hush up. Get your things out of that motel and move right in with me and say not another word." Gucci picks up the straw and snorts a line, takes a big sip of his drink and Marsha does the same. Then both hit hands, laugh and say, "Hey!"

Gucci gets a call on his cell phone. It's one of his favorite clients. Gucci answers his cell phone. He looks at the name in his cell phone, answers and says, "Hello Mr. dead." The man says, "Now listen at you, why you want to say something like that?" Gucci says, "You know why I said it with your dead behind. I don't even know why I even fool with you because all you do is sleep." Marsha start laughing at what Gucci was saying. The man asks, "Can you meet me at Big Momma House?" Gucci says, "No I am not going to meet you, you meet me." The man asks, "Where?" Gucci says, "In Alligator Alley in about an hour see you later alligator." The man says, "Ok." Gucci says, "Wait a minute, what you suppose to say?" The man says, "After while crocodile." Gucci says, "And don'ts you forget it." Gucci hangs up the phone.

An hour later, the man is driving very slowly down Alligator Alley which is a dark dirt road leading into the forest trees. It's very dark and he's looking down the road as through his eyes are about to pop out of his head. Then all of a sudden Gucci jumps out of the bushes from the road right in front of the man's car, bends over with his head between his legs and his butt facing the bright lights on his car. The man throws on breaks. Gucci straightens up and starts to laugh. Gucci gets in the car. The man is shaking with his eyes about to pop out of his head. Gucci looks at him and says, "Fool snap out of it, lets go." The man is stilling looking at Gucci shaking. Gucci says, "Drive Fool!" The man eyes still looking like they're about to pop out of his head drives off.

In the mean time at Big Momma's House a prostitute comes in with her date whom happens to be a Midget. Big Momma is behind the counter but all she could see is the prostitute. So Big Momma says, "Hi Baby, are you meeting someone here or your date hasn't come in yet?" The prostitute says, "My date is here." Big Momma looks at her strange like saying here where? The prostitute points down at the Midget. Big Momma stands up and looks down across the counter and sees the Midget deck down in a three piece loud green suit and hat with a feather on it and quickly sit back down. She looks at the prostitute trying to keep from laughing and says, "How many hours do you want?" The prostitute says, "Two hours." Big Momma says, "That will be twenty dollars Baby." The prostitute looks down at the Midget and he takes his wallet out and hands her twenty dollars. Big Momma takes the money and says, "Thank you Baby, room number four." So the couple starts walking to their room.

It's Sunday and the choir is up singing. Eunice is sitting in the audience looking around to see if she sees Marsha and spots Marsha's Mom with her head down as though she's at a funeral. Kathy (Marsha's sister) has her arms around her mother as though she's consoling her. Eunice turns her head back around with a puzzled look on her face as thinking what is going on. After the choir finishes singing, Pastor Williams comes to the roster with his bible in his hand. He places his bible on the roster, opens it and says, "Giving honor to our Lord and Savior, Jesus Christ, to all the Elders and Ministers of the gospel, to our Deacons, Mothers and to the entire congregation. I am going to speak to you briefly today, because it lay on my heart that somebody needs urgent prayer this morning.

The title of my message today is, "Come unto me", taken from the book of Matthew 11: 28. Jesus said, "Come to me, all you who are exhausted and weighted down beneath your burdens, and I will give you rest. Jesus spoke to men who were desperately trying to be good, who were driven to weariness and to despair. His invitation is to those who are exhausted with the search for the truth. Jesus said, "Come unto me all who are weighted down beneath your burdens. It's the kinds of burdens that bind us so hard that we can't do anything for ourselves.

The doctor calls it depression. You become so depressed until it seems as though you can't find your way out. But I am here to tell you today that God is right there with His hands stretched out waiting for you to come to Him. Jesus said if you come to Him, He will give you rest. Now I am saying to you, those who feel like your burdens are too heavy and you need rest, I ask you to come to the altar. I am going to ask Minister Gibson to come and lead us in prayer."

The choir stands and began to sing the song, "Come to Jesus." The Pastor Looks around and have James to call Alter call.

James gets up and comes to the roster and the Pastor sits down. James says, "If anyone feels that your soul needs rest, come. If you are heavy burden come, if you need help in your finances come, and if you have a child that has lost their way come." Kathy immediately looks at her mother and helps her up out of her seat. They both start walking towards the Alter. Mrs. Green burst out in tears as she stands at the Alter because she has Marsha on her mind. Kathy consoles her as they both stand before the Alter as others followed and gathered around the Alter. Eunice kept watching Mrs. Green sensing something is greatly wrong.

After service Eunice made her way out of the door to catch up with Kathy and her mother. Eunice spots them outside and makes her ways to them. Eunice shakes both of their hands and says, "Hello Mrs. Green and Kathy, how's everyone doing?" Kathy says, "I am doing fine, but Momma is kind of worried about Marsha." Mrs. Green holds her head down trying to hold back the tears. Eunice says, "If you don't mine me asking, what's wrong?" Kathy says, "Well I guest it's nothing wrong with telling you you're going to find out sooner or later. Momma is worried about Marsha. Marsha packed up her things and left without a word. We haven't heard from her since she left and Momma is worried about how she's doing. Momma suspects that Marsha is on drugs sleeping in the streets somewhere and may get hurt." Eunice hugs Mrs. Green and says, "Don't worry Mrs. Green, one day after work I'll see if I could catch up with her. You know Marsha and I are very close. I'll let you know if I find out where she is." Eunice kisses Mrs. Green on the cheek and gives her a hug.

Later that Sunday evening Marsha is at Gucci's apartment setting up the dinner table getting ready to serve dinner. Gucci is dressed in plain clothes looking very handsome enters the dinning room and sits at the dinner table. Marsha starts bringing the food placing it on the table. Gucci looks and says, "Girl look at that." Marsha smiles and goes back in the kitchen and brings out the home made biscuits and set them on the table. Gucci snaps his fingers and waves his hands in the air and says, "Little Miss Muffin you made home made biscuits for the Queen?" Marsha laughs and says, "Yes I did your Majesty." Gucci snaps his fingers again and says, "Alright girl." Marsha looks at him laughing and says, "Gucci you so crazy let me go in here and finish bringing everything out."

After Marsha finishes setting the table and sits down, Gucci gets ready to dig in and Marsha says, "Gucci wait, lets give thanks." Gucci says, "Oh this is serious." Then he bows his head and Marsha gives thanks to the Lord in prayer. Gucci starts digging in loading his plate with food and says, "Girl you be having some serious Sundays." Marsha says, "Well Gucci this is what goes on at my house on Sundays. After Church we sit around the dinner table, we always give thanks to God. We talk about how we enjoyed the service at church." Then Marsha starts to say something else and puts her hand over her face and burst out in tears, because she remembers her up bringing from a Christian home. Gucci sadly looks on.

The same day at the Green's house, Mrs. Green is in her bedroom still dressed in her church clothes sitting on her bed looking into space. Kathy is setting the dinner table and realizes that Mrs. Green has not come out of her room. So she goes to her mother's room and she sees her mother just sitting on her bed looking into space quietly. Kathy walks up to her and says, "Momma what's wrong?" Mrs. Green drops her head in tears. Kathy sits beside her and puts her arms around her mother and says, "Momma I know you're probably thinking about Marsha but she's going to be alright. Momma you done your best in teaching us the right way and I know the Lord hears your cry.

You taught us Momma that if we believe, God will protect us and I believe He will bring her safely back home." Mrs. Green with tears falling from her face says to Kathy, "You always acted like my baby even though you're the oldest. Why couldn't she be like you? Marsha always was more outgoing than you." Kathy says, "But Momma that doesn't mean that she's a bad person, sometimes people just get with the wrong crowd." Mrs. Green hugs Kathy and says, "Thank you baby." Then Mrs. Green looks up and says, "Lord help me to bear this pain. Please keep a watch over her Lord and bring her back to me safely." Then they both hug each other in tears.

Later that day Marsha calls Eunice on her cell phone. Eunice is in the kitchen putting the dishes away. Her mother is in the living room reading her bible. Eunice's cell phone rings. Eunice picks up the phone and says, "Hello." Marsha says, "Hey Boo, what going on?" Eunice says, "You are what's going on. Your mother is worried sick about you. Why haven't you called her?" Marsha says, "Well I haven't gotten around to it yet. I first had to get my living conditions resolved, and also I was trying to get up the nerve to call her. Did you see her in church today?" Eunice says, "Yes I did and she looked terrible. I spoke with her and your sister after service and Kathy told me what was going on. So Marsha, tell me what is going on with you. Why did you move out so quickly without telling anyone?" Marsha got quiet. Eunice says, "Hello, are you still there?" Marsha hesitates and says, "Yes I am here." Eunice says, "Well answer me. You know you can tell me anything. We are buddies remember?" Marsha says, "Boo now you know it had to be for a good reason for me to up and leave home like that. I have some issues that led from one thing to another. I was trying to deal with the situation that I was in and lost my job. Momma caught up with me and I couldn't handle her disappointment in me."

Eunice says, "I can understand that, but yet you need to call her and let her know that you're alright. You can start by telling her the exact thing that you are telling me now." Marsha says, "I will Eunice but I got to get myself together first. This is the first time that I've been sober this week, I quest because it's Sunday. I thought about Momma while we were eating dinner." Eunice says, "We who?" Marsha says, "My friend Gucci." Eunice says, "Oh, you have a room mate?" Marsha says, "Yes, I had checked into a motel and Gucci offered me to stay here in his apartment. He has a big beautiful two bedroom apartment we get along very well." Eunice says, "That's nice. Maybe one day I get a chance to meet him and also see the apartment.

Now Marsha I am not trying to get religious on you but you know how we were raised up in the church and what our parents taught us. I am not saying that I am better than you because I am still in the church, but it does come a time when we have to make choices and a lot of times we make the wrong choices that we think are the right ones given the situation that we are in. I believe that this is what happened to you but even though you may have made a bad choice due to your state of mind at the time, God will forgive you and make you new all over again." Marsha gets angry and says, "There you go Miss Goody Too Shoes! You don't know how I felt and how I feel now. You haven't gone through what I went through. It's easy for you to say that to me because you're on the outside looking in!" Eunice says, "I am sorry that you feel that way, but I believe that God can change any situation that we may be in through prayer and you know that. I am not telling you something that you don't already know." Marsha begins to cry over the phone. Eunice says to Marsha, "Don't cry Marsha, but me being weak is not going to help your situation, somebody has to be strong. You wouldn't have called me if you didn't think you needed someone to talk to and that's what I am doing, talking to you. So you dry up those tears and get in your head that you are going to fight this thing with the Lord's help. Now look up towards the hills where you know where your help is coming from. I love you and please, don't forget to call your Mom." Marsha dries up her tears and says, "Okay Boo talk to you later." Eunice quickly says, Wait, I am going to save this number in my phone, but what is your address?" Marsha gives Eunice her address. Eunice writes it down and says, "Okay Marsha I'll be calling you to check up on you and if I decide to come over I'll call you first bye, bye." Eunice hangs up the phone. (*We must be ready to speak in time.*)

It's Monday morning and James is in his office talking to Edward the troubled student who home he visited. He says to Edward, "Your teacher tells me that you are improving tremendously in class. No more sleeping and that you are keeping up with your studies. That's good to hear Edward. It makes me very proud of you." Edward looking all fresh and happy says, "That's because I have my own bedroom now." James says, "You mean you all have a new place?" Edward says, yes and my Mom has a job." James says, "That's great news Edward. Let me look at your files a minute to see if your Mom has up dated your personal information." James looks in Edward folder that he has in front of him on his desk. James says, "Oh I see she did call in and updated everything, that perfect.

So how are you enjoying your new place?" Edward says, "I love it. I have new friends in the neighborhood and Momma dress different now." James says, "I think I know what you mean. Maybe I might stop by one day to check on you and your Mom, how about that?" Edward smiles and says, "Okay." James says, "It's been good talking to you Edward. Now you hang in there, alright?" Edward says, "Okay Mr. Gibson." James says, "Good, now you can return to class." Edward gets up out of his chair and leaves going back to class. Immediately James reaches in his pocket for his address book and writes down Edward's address and phone number. Then he smiles to himself thinking of how Edward's Mom may look now. Then he catches himself and closes the folder and goes to the file cabinet and replaces Edwards's files.

Later that evening James is driving home and about half way he starts thinking about Edward's Mom and how she may look now. James pulls into the gas station and parks. James takes his phone book out of his pocket and looks at Edward's address. James pulls back out of the gas station and proceeds to look for Edward's address. When he gets to the street, he slowly drives looking for the house number. He spots the house number and parks. James gets out of his car and walks slowly looking around and rings the door bell. Edward and his Mom (Miss Spencer) are having dinner. Ms. Spencer hears the door bell ring and goes to answer the door. Ms. Spencer opens the door. James is shocked the way Ms. Spencer looks. She's wearing her own hair which is black, long and beautiful, very little makeup and she has on a lovely blouse and jeans. James is standing there staring at her speechless. Ms. Spencer says, "Hi Mr. Gibson, come in."

James goes in and Ms. Spencer directs him to the living room and Edward is still eating dinner and spots James and says, "Hi Mr. Gibson." James turns around and speaks to Edward. As they approach the living room, James says, "I hope I am not disturbing your dinner." Ms. Spencer says, "Have a seat. No you're not disturbing anything I was about finished eating any way. So what brings you by this evening, I hope Edward is behaving in class." James says, "No Edward is doing fine I just was delighted to hear some good things about his new home. Edward had a big smile on his face telling me about the move you all had made."

So Ms. Spencer began to talk about the move they made and how he played a big part in turning her life around. But James was staring so deeply at her until her words was fading in and out of his ears as though he was in a trance. Ms. Spencer had stopped talking but James's mind had gone off in a short trance. Ms. Spencer looking at him strangely said, "Mr. Gibson, Mr. Gibson, are you alright?" James come out of it and stands up and says, I better be going I guess my wife is wondering why I am running a little late." *(Some you must pity and fear at the same time, hating the garment stained by the flesh.)* Ms. Spencer stands up and says, "Well it was nice of you to stop by." They walked to the door and said good night.

On the way driving home, James couldn't seem to shake Ms. Spencer off of his mind so much so until he almost ran off of the road. When he got home his kids ran up to him saying, "Daddy, Daddy." James picks them up and kissed them. His wife was in the kitchen clearing off the table where the kids had eaten. So she came out of the kitchen and saw James playing with the kids and said, "Okay that's enough it times for you all to go to bed. Now say good night to Daddy." The kids said goodnight to James and both of them ran off to bed. His wife then looked at James and said, "Well I quest it's a first for everything." James looked at her with a guilty look on his face and said, "What do you mean by that?" She just turned around and said, "I kept your dinner warm in the oven. When ever you get ready to eat I'll fix your plate." James says, wait a minute I asked you what you meant by that!" But she ignored him and kept walking towards the kitchen. James rubbed his head and went to their bedroom.

Later that night Gucci and Marsha are riding in a cab going to meet a client at Big Momma's House. Gucci says to Marsha, "We're going to have some fun tonight. You just do what ever I tell you." Marsha says, "Wait a minute, if this includes me I want to know what's going on." Gucci says, "I suppose to meet Poppa Joe at Big Momma's and he told me to bring an extra lady which is you. He already paid for the room. Now I don't really want to be bothered with Poppa Joe because everything is just in his mind. He's though dealing. Just follow me." They reach Big Momma's House.

Gucci tells the cab driver to stay parked and wait they'll be right out. The cab driver says, "Okay." Gucci and Marsha get out of the cab and rushes in Big Momma's House. Big Momma is behind the counter. She sees them come in and says, "Hello girls what's it going to be like?" Gucci says, "The man is in room six waiting on us. He said he already paid for the room." Big Momma says, "Oh yes he's expecting you two. Just go right down the hall to room six." Gucci says, "Thank you Momma." So they go down the hall and Gucci knocks on the door.

Poppa Joe asks, "Who is it?" Gucci says, "Who you think it is Lavern and Shirley?" Poppa Joe cracks the door a little and sees it's Gucci and let them in. Poppa Joe has red and white flower trunks on and looks like he's about eighty years old. Marsha looks at Gucci and says, "No you wouldn't Gucci that's murder." Gucci says, "Girl you so crazy, come on and let's get started." Marsha says, "Get started doing what?" Gucci says, "That's alright." Then Gucci tells Poppa Joe to lie on his stomach in the bed. Poppa Joe starts to shake with excitement and lies down in the bed on his stomach like Gucci told him to do. Gucci rubs him on his back and down his legs. Poppa Joe starts shaking more and more and falls asleep. Gucci goes through his pant's pockets and gets his wallet, and takes the cash out.

Gucci says, "My, my, my girl looks at all this money." Gucci puts the money in his bosom and grabs Marsha by the hand and says, "Girl lets go!" Marsha looks at the man and Gucci pulls her arm and says, "Let's go!" Then they both rush out of the room down the hall. About half way Gucci tells Marsha softly, "Now walk normal so Big Momma doesn't suspect anything." Marsha says, "Okay." (*Influence plays a big role in lives today*) So they slow down and when they reached the front desk Gucci says to Big Momma, "Thank you see you next time." Big Momma says, "Okay girls take care."

When they got outside, Gucci burst out laughing and start running to the cab. Marsha runs behind him and they both get in the cab laughing like crazy. Gucci still laughing tells the cab driver to take off.

The next evening James is off from work on his way home. He looks at his watch to see what time it is. It's about 5: 30 pm. He's thinking about Ms. Spencer. He makes a right turn and goes to Ms. Spencer's house. After he arrives, he sits in his car for a little while with his head on the steering wheel contemplating whether or not he should get out and go to the door. He finally gets out of the car and walks to the door and rings the door bell. Ms. Spencer comes to the door and looks through the peep hole and sees that it's James and opens the door. Ms. Spencer says, "Hi, come in." James comes in and stares at her deeply. She looks into his eyes as though she could read his mind. She knows he didn't just stop by. She smiles and says, "Come have a seat." James sits down on the sofa.

Ms. Spencer looks around at her son Edward. Edward is sitting at the dinner table doing his home work. Ms. Spencer tells Edward to finish his home work in his room. Edward says, "Ok mom", and he gathers his papers and on his way to his room he speaks to James. Then Ms. Spencer sits down on the love seat across from James and says, "It's nice of you to stop by again. Is everything alright, Edward hasn't gotten in any kind of trouble at school I hope." James says, "No it's nothing like that. I just........I am sorry I'd better be going." James gets up and starts towards the door shaking his head not knowing what else to say. Ms. Spencer gets up and walks behind him and says, "Wait a minute." James turns around and she gets closer to him, looking him deeply in his eyes and says, "If it wasn't about Edward then why did you stop by?" James drops his head and says, "I don't know, I guess I wanted to see you again." Then he holds his head up to see her reaction.

Ms. Spencer smiles and says, "You're new at this kind of thing aren't you?" James looks deep in her eyes and says, "Am I that obvious?" Ms. Spencer moves closer to him as though she wants him to kiss her. James puts his hands on her face, pulls her up to him and deeply kisses her. James catches himself and says, "I'd better be going." Ms. Spencer says, "I understand." James asks her can he see her again. Ms. Spencer looks at him and says, "You know that this is a dead end." James just looks at her and says, "Take care" and opens the door and leaves.

Later James gets home. His wife is in the kitchen finishing up dinner. The kids are on the living room floor watching cartoons. James walks in. The kids see him and runs up to him saying, "Daddy, Daddy!" James hugs them and says, "How are you little monsters doing?" By that time his wife comes out of the kitchen. James leaves the kids and walks up to her and says, "Hi babe" and kisses her on the cheek. James holds her in his arms very tight about to cry. She asks him, "What's this all about?" James just looks sadly at her and says, "I just realize how much I love you." His wife looks at him with compassion and says, "I love you too" and they hug each other.

Later that evening, Mrs. Green gets a call from Marsha. She and Kathy are at the dinner table having supper. The phone rings in the kitchen. Kathy says to her mother, "I'll get it!" So she jumps up from the table and answers the phone. Kathy says, "Hello." Marsha says, "Hey Boo." Kathy screams and says, "Marsha is this you?!" Mrs. Green looks up and grabs her cheeks with her eyes stretched and mouth open and says, "Is that my Baby?!" Mrs. Green jumps up from the table excited, tears begin to roll down her face and she grabs the phone from Kathy and says, Hi Baby, where are you, are you alright?!" Marsha begins to cry and says, "Momma slow down, I am doing fine. How are you doing?" Mrs. Green says, "Baby I've been worried wondering where you are, what was you doing, were you in some kind of trouble or something. I just didn't know what to think. Baby please come home, we can work it out what ever it may be. I miss you so much and Kathy does too!" Marsha (trying to hold back her tears) says, "Momma I am doing fine. I am sorry the way I left. Mom I didn't want to disrespect you like that anymore in our home. Mom, just give me a little more time. Momma I need you so much, but I don't know how to tell you. Momma I know that you're praying for me or else I wouldn't have called." Mrs. Green says, "Baby you know I am praying and I believe that the Lord is answering my prayers. He let me hear from my Baby. Baby please come home, we can work it out. You know how you were raised in the church and I believe that the Lord will forgive you for what ever may be the case."

Marsha crying says, "Momma I believe, now Momma I am going to hang up now, I love you." Mrs. Green pleads, Baby please don't hang up, let me hear your voice a little longer, please!" Crying, Marsha hangs up the phone. Mrs. Green still holding the phone pleading and Kathy gets up from the table and takes the phone out of Mrs. Green's hand. Kathy puts the phone up to her ear and hears the dial tone. She puts the phone back on the receiver and consoles her mother. Kathy tells her mother to sit down in the chair, and Mrs. Green as she is sitting down says, "Lord, please take care of my Baby."

Then later that night at Big Momma's a young girl and a man drives up. The man tells the girl that a man called Henry is going to meet her there. She is to go in the room with him and He is going to give her two hundred dollars. The girl asks, "What I am I to do for him to give me that kind of money?" He tells her not to worry about that, just do what he tells her to do. The man then tells her to get out of the car and he'll be back to pick her up, and she had better not mess up or she will have to deal with him. So the girl gets out of the car as though she's afraid. The man pulls off and she goes into Big Momma's place.

Big Momma is sitting behind the desk checking in a couple. After Big Momma checks them in she tells them their room number. Then the young girl walks up to the desk. Then the girl begins to cry as though she's afraid. Big Momma asks, "What's wrong, are you lost or what?" The girl says, "I am suppose to meet someone here name Henry." Big Momma says, "Are you sure you have the right place?" The girl says. "Yes I am sure." Big Momma says. "Well if you do have the right place, I think you're too young to come in here. How old are you?" The girl says, "I am fifteen years old." Big Momma stretches her eyes and says, "First of all you're too young to come in here, and where are your parents?" The girl says, "They are in Texas." Big Momma asks, "Who are you here with, a relative or something?" The girl says, "No I ran away from home." Big Momma asks, "Who brought you here?" The girl says, Mr. Flash." Big Momma asks, "Do you know what this so called Mr. Flash is about?" The girl says, "He's the one who offered me a place to stay." Big Momma says, "Well let me tell you something Sweaty, this is going to go on and on and on.

He's going to take your money every time. Things are going to get ruff. If you don't do what he says, he's going to start beating you every time you refuse. He is going to treat you as though he owns you. You don't know what you are getting into. Take it from me I know his kind Sweaty. You need to get your little behind back to Texas to your parents and try to work things out rather than to run. These are some mean streets. What's happening at home could never compare to what's going to happen to you out here in these streets.

These girls come in here all wish that they could start all over again. Some can't stop because they need the money to support their drug habit; some do it because they dropped out of school at an early age and feel that they can't get a decent job because they don't have a high school diploma. Sweaty you have a chance to do better. Go on back home to your parents and get an education so you wouldn't have to stoop this low. Sweaty listen, I am going to give you some money to get back home and I want you to get out of here as fast as you can!" (*Some must be argued out of their error while there is still time.*)

Big Momma reaches in her bosom to get the money and counts out the money. Big Momma hands the girl the money and says; "Now here's enough to get you back to Texas, cab fare and little something for food. Now I am going to call my cab driver to come and pick you up. Do what I tell you Sweaty. I don't know why I am doing this for you. It must be your parent's prayers. But anyway let me call Jimmy to pick you up." Big Momma picks up the phone and calls the Cab. She ask Jimmy the cab driver where is he she needs him ASAP. The cab driver says he's just ten blocks away and that he'll be there in fifteen minutes.

When the cab arrives the young girl hugs Big Momma in tears and thanks Big Momma. Big Momma trying to hold her tears back, tells the girl to run to the cab. Then as Big Momma watches her getting in the cab she remembers that she didn't even get the girl's name.

James stops by Ms. Spencer's house that evening after work. James and Ms. Spencer are in her bedroom. After lying with her, he's sitting on the side of the bed talking to her. James tells her he can't help himself anymore and that it seems as though he's driven to her. Ms. Spencer tells him she's beginning to feel the same way. She said she had hoped that he would stop by. James looks at her in amazement and tells her maybe that's what drew him there.

Ms. Spencer sits up in the bed as though she was thinking very hard. James asks her is there something wrong. Ms. Spencer tells him that she knows that she would have to face the day when they could no longer see each other. James reaches up and pulls her back down in bed and tells her to just enjoy the moment. She looks at him and tells him that she certainly will and they kiss.

Later that evening James walks in the door of his home. His wife is sitting in the living room. As he closes the door slowly, he turns around and says, "Hi Baby, Daddy's home. Sorry I am late but I was talking to the coach and watching the kids practice baseball." His wife asks him why he didn't call and let her know that because she was worried that something had happened to him. James reaches and pulls her up from the couch and hugs her saying that he's sorry it won't happen again. But his wife has a suspicious look on her face. James looks at her and tells her to give him a kiss and they kiss.

The next day James is in his office at work sitting thinking about what had happened between him and Ms. Spencer. He was like he was in a trance. One of the secretaries walked in looking at him and says, "Mr. Gibson look like your mind is way out there." James catches himself and tells her he was just thinking about something. She laughs and tells him he had another note from a teacher about a troubling student. She hands him the note. James takes the note and tells her thank you. The secretary smiles and tells him he's welcome and walks out of his office. James reads the note and places it on his desk.

After James gets off from work he's on his way home, but he turns around and head to Ms. Spencer's house. James rings the door bell. Ms. Spencer opens the door. He asks her where her son was. She tells him he's in his room doing his home work. James grabs her and head for her bed room. He locks the door and they begin to kiss. James starts to undress and so does she. He kisses her and kisses her all the way to her bed. They make love like two dogs in heat.

Later when James gets home, he sits in his car thinking what to tell his wife because he knows he's late getting there. He's even later than the last time but he knows he can't just sit in his car all night. So he gets out of his car and enters his house. There she was sitting in the same spot waiting. James says in a lower tone of voice, "Hi Babe." In a calm and sarcastic way she says, "Tell me you had a flat tire or you miss and left your cell phone at the job that's why you're late. You couldn't call me to let me know? James I know you, you can't hide anything from me and you know that. Now I am not going to argue with you, but I hope it's not another woman." James just stands there looking, not knowing what to say. His wife gets up and walks away to the bedroom.

It's Sunday morning and James's wife tells him it time to get up and get dressed for church. James rolls over in bed and tells her he don't think he's going. She asks him why he's not going. James lies and tells her he's not feeling well. She asks him what is wrong. James tells her that he's just not feeling well. She tells him he knows that the Pastor is going to be looking for him. But James just turns over in the bed and ignores her. She becomes angry and says, "James you never miss church what is going on with you?!" But James still wouldn't say anything. So she storms out of the room and slams the door. James then turns over on his back, looks up at the ceiling, puts his hands over his face and began to cry because he knows he has hurt his wife.

After his wife and the kids are at church, James calls Ms. Spencer and tells her that he's thinking about moving out of his house for a while. Ms. Spencer asks him where he is going to go. James tells her he probably get a motel some place. Ms. Spencer tells him he could come and stay with her. He tells her he doesn't want to get her involved no more than he has already. Ms. Spencer tells him that this was bound to happen and the way they feel about each other wasn't going to be hidden much longer. But to make sure that this is what he want to do. James tells her that he cares very deeply about his wife and the kids and he knows that it is not his wife's fault, it's him. He tells her that he can't seem to stay away from her. Something seems to be drawing him to her, and can't seem to hide it anymore. So he has decided to pack some of his things before she comes home from church. Ms. Spencer asks him does he want her to pick him up. James tells her that he has his own car and that his wife drove her car. Ms. Spencer asks him is he coming to stay with her. James says yes. Ms. Spencer tells him that she will be waiting. James tells her that he will see her soon and hangs up the phone.

When James wife comes home she notices that James's car is not there. She immediately parks and gets out of the car, lets the kids out of the car and rushes inside the house. She tells the kids to go to their room and take off their church clothes. Then she goes to her room to get undressed and notice that some of the dresser draws were left partly opened. So she goes over to the dressers and looks in each drawer and notice that James's underwear, t-shirts and socks were gone. Then she rushes over to the closet and sees that some of his pants and shoes were gone. She grabs her face in anguish and falls on her bed crying saying, "Lord no!"

The next day Brenda (James's wife) drives over Mrs. Gibson's house (James Mother). Brenda gets out of her car and rings the door bell. Mrs. Gibson is sitting in the living room reading her bible. Mrs. Gibson hears the door bell ring and answers the door. She sees that it's Brenda and says, "What a surprise, I didn't suspect that it was you! Come on in and have a seat." As Brenda enter the house she just burst out and starts to cry. Mrs. Gibson stunned says, "Baby what's wrong?" Brenda walks over to the living room sits down crying. Mrs. Gibson sits down by her and says, "Tell me, what is wrong?" Brenda says, "I think James has left me." Mrs. Gibson says, "What do you mean, left you? When did all this happen? Was something going on between you two and you all kept things hid?" Brenda still with tears falling from her eyes says, "Mom I don't know things happened so fast. He had been coming home late and the last time I just told him that I hoped it wasn't another woman. The next morning he said he wasn't going to church because he wasn't feeling well and when I got home from church he was gone." Mrs. Gibson said, "What do you mean he was gone? Did he take anything with him?" Brenda says, "Yes he took some of his clothes and shoes." Mrs. Gibson holds her to her chest crying saying, "Baby the Lord is able, don't you worry, we just got to pray for whatever it is, and the Lord will fix it."

About two days later James is in his office at school in deep thoughts about his wife. He decides to call her. So he gets up from his desk and shuts the door. He sits back down at his desk and calls her from his cell phone. Brenda is sitting on the bed thinking of him. The phone rings in her room. It's James. James tells her that he is sorry for everything that has happened. He tells her that he just needs some space to think things over. He tells her that he hated to keep lying to her about everything and that he still loves her. Brenda asks him what is it?! He tells her that he's been unfaithful and that it's nothing that he can do about it, it just happened. Brenda tells him that he needs to come back home and maybe they can work things out. James tells her he doesn't want to talk about it right now and that he will call her later. Brenda tries to keep him on the phone and says, "You know I love you, don't do this please." James just hangs up the phone. Brenda begins to cry.

When James got off from work, he went to Ms. Spencer's house and they are sitting down at the table with her son eating dinner. Her son asks James is he going to be staying with them. Ms. Spencer tells her son to just wait and see. Her son says, "I just want to know if he's going to be my daddy, I like him a lot." Ms. Spencer smiles and says, "Eat your food Edward." Edward starts back to eating his dinner.

Over to James house Brenda and the kids are doing the same, having dinner. John asks his mother why is she so sad. Is something wrong with daddy?" Brenda asks him why he asks that question. John tells her that it's because he haven't seen his daddy in a long time. His little girl says, "Yea, where is daddy momma?" Brenda trying to hold back the tears says, "Daddy may be gone for a while, ok?" The son says, "I miss daddy momma." The little girl says, "Me too." Brenda just drops her head.

The next day Brenda waits until she thinks James is off from work, drives to his school and parks so James doesn't she her. She watches as James enters the school's parking lot and gets in his car. James doesn't even look around he just gets in his car and drives off. Brenda follows him at a distance. Soon James turns and drives up to Ms. Spencer's house. Brenda stops down the street but she has a good look at what house he parked at. She waits about five minutes assuming that he has gotten out of his car and went in the house. Then she slowly drives past the house to get a good look at the house James entered.

The next day while James was at work, Brenda returns to the house where she saw James entered. She rings the door bell and

Ms. Spencer answers the door. Ms. Spencer says, "Yes may I help you." Brenda says, "My name is Mrs. Gibson, James's wife." Ms. Spencer shocked, hesitates at first. Brenda asks, "Can I come in?" Ms. Spencer says, "Sure come in and have a seat." Brenda goes in and Ms. Spencer directs her to the living room. Brenda sits on the couch and Ms. Spencer sits down in the love seat. Ms. Spencer says, "You don't have to tell me I think I know what this is about. I didn't want this to happen, it just happened. I knew James was a married man from the beginning and I told him that this was a dead end.

But he was very persistent." Brenda says, "Well, what has happened has happened. I just want you to give him back to me." Ms. Spencer laughs and says, "Give him back to you, you mean I actually have him?" Brenda says, "What I mean is you have the power to do so. James is a good man and he's a minister of our church. I know that he knows better. Temptation is something that we may all as Christians have to face but, giving in to temptation is where we fall in to sin." Ms. Spencer becomes a little heated up and says, "Don't you come in here preaching to me, save that for James!" Brenda keeps her calm and says, "I love him and the children misses him, this is all I know to do is to come to you and I plead with you to let him go. It may hurt him, but you know yourself that it's wrong. Put yourself in my place, how would you feel if your husband or boyfriend left you for another woman?"

Then Brenda begins to cry and says, "Please help me, it not only him, this is destroying a whole family. You don't have much to lose. I know that it is just a fling with you and you can take him or leave him. But I love him and I need him. You are a mother, think of what this is doing to his kids, they miss him. I have to deal with their questions of, "When is daddy coming home?" Doesn't that mean anything to you? I prayed to the Lord to bring him back to me, so the coal is on your head. I thank you for inviting me in your house, now I am going to go, goodbye." Brenda heads for the door and leaves. As Brenda shuts the door behind her, Ms. Spencer walks behind her and locks the door. Then she leans with her back against the door and drops her head.

Brenda gets in her car and decides to go over to her mother-in-law, Mrs. Gibson. When she gets there and goes in the house. She starts to cry and tells Mrs. Gibson what she did concerning Ms. Spencer. Mrs. Gibson consoling her says, "Baby you did a dangerous thing going over there. It could have turned out to be a big argument and someone could have gotten hurt." Brenda says, "Momma I just felt numb. Listening to the kids asking about their father just tore me up inside."

Later that night, James and Ms. Spencer are in bed talking. Ms. Spencer asks him do he love her. James tells her that she knows he does. Then he asks her, "Why, what's wrong?" Ms. Spencer says, "I just wanted to know. You know it could be just a fling that you have for me." James says, "What do you mean just a fling?" Ms. Spencer says, "What I mean is, our relationship, where is it going?" James says, "We will just have to see." Ms. Spencer says, "While we are doing that, I lot of people may be hurt." James says, "I know, but I just can't help it right now." Then they kiss deeply.

The next morning after James had left for work, Ms. Spencer's conscience began to bother her. Thinking about what Brenda had said to her and how sad it was to see her cry and plead with her concerning James. She begins to cry knowing what she had to do and also that she was falling in love with James.

It's Saturday afternoon and James is standing in the living room calling out to Edward because he wants to take him to play basketball one-on-one. Edward runs out of his room dressed to play basketball. James asks, "Are you ready my man?" Edward smile and says, "Yes Mr. Gibson." James smiles and rubs Edward on the head and says, "Let's go." Then James calls out to Ms. Spencer, "Betty we're leaving." Ms. Spencer says as she comes out of the kitchen, "Ok James you all enjoy yourselves. By what time do you think you'll be back?" James says, "Right before dinner time." Ms. Spencer kisses James on the cheek and says, "See you then. Bye Edward." Edward smiles and says, "Bye Mom."

After they leave Ms. Spencer sits down in the living room and holds her head down and cries because she knows that one day she's going to have to make a decision about her and James. She wants him to stay but at the same time she's haunted by what James's wife said to her about James's children missing him and what affect the same thing might happen to her son if he gets to attached to James.

Brenda (James's wife) is home watching television in the living room. The kids are running from room to room playing hide and go seek. Every time one finds the other they scream and start laughing. Brenda began to get irritated from the kids screaming. Then the kid's takes off behind each other running through the living room. One was trying to catch the other screaming at the same time. Brenda loses her temper and yells at them saying, "Look, stop all that noise, don't you see that I am trying to hear the TV! Are you all crazy!? Go to your rooms both of you, and I don't want to hear a sound!" They both stand there froze looking at Brenda with their eyes stretched like they never seen their mother look like that before. Then Brenda raises her voice again and says, "Did you all hear me!?" They sadly went to their rooms. Then Brenda catches herself and takes a deep breath. She puts her hands up to her face and lays her head back on the chair and thinks for a little while. She realizes that she was just thinking about James leaving her and should not have taken it out on the kids. So she calls them to come to her. Both kids came out of their rooms but stayed a distance as though they were afraid. Brenda smiles at them and opens her arms and says, "Come on Momma is sorry." They run into her arms. Then Brenda says, "I didn't mean to yell at my babies, Momma love her babies."

The next evening on a Sunday James and Ms. Spencer is sitting in the living room on the sofa watching TV holding hands. James says, "Don't you kind of miss Edward?" Ms. Spencer doesn't answer because the coal is burning on her head thinking about James's wife. James looks at her and says, "Didn't you hear me?" Ms. Spencer catches herself and says, "No what did you say?" James says, "Is something wrong? You seem to be out of it." Ms. Spencer says, "I guess I was kind of." James asks, what were you thinking about so deeply? It must be very serious." Ms. Spencer says, "James I don't think you are really in love with me. I think that you are just infatuated with me." James says, "Infatuated, no I care a lot about you." Ms. Spencer says, "Do you love me?" James says, "Yes, I love you." Ms. Spencer says, "Do you love your wife?" James says, "Yes I love my wife. She hasn't done anything to me for me not to love her. She's the mother of my children." Ms. Spencer says, "James, you can't love two people at the same time. Are you through with the relationship between you and her?" James says, I don't know, all I can think about is you right now. I know that I enjoy being with you. It seems like it's a feeling that over takes me. I can't help myself. I can't think about what's wrong or right any more. Let's just play everything by ear and see what happens." Ms. Spencer says, "James Edward is becoming very fun of you and I don't want him to be hurt again. You have gotten us on the right track now and I thank you for that. I know that I haven't been the best mom for him in the past but I am trying to make up for that. I am going to have to do whatever it takes to make up to him while he's still young."

James says, "Where did all this come from all of a sudden? I thought things were kind of good between us." Ms. Spencer says, "You know the type of woman that I am. I know men. You probably haven't experienced many women in your life." James says, "Wait a minute where is this going? Betty please, I need you right now. Maybe I might go back to my wife and maybe I won't, but let's enjoy the time that we have, please." Ms. Spencer looks at James and sadly says, "James you don't know what you are doing. I know you don't." James doesn't know that he has given Ms. Spencer the answer that she was expecting. So Ms. Spencer just says, "James, whatever happens, take care of yourself." James just grabs her and kiss her and says, "Don't worry things are going to be alright."

It's Monday and James is at work. Ms. Spencer has made up her mind about her and James's relationship. Ms. Spencer goes in her room and began to pack James clothes. With tears falling from her eyes, she takes James luggage and sits them by the front door.

She called her friend name (Bruce) to tell him what her plans were. Bruce answers the phone. Ms. Spencer says, "Hi Bruce this is Betty, it's been a long time." Bruce says, "Yes it has. How have you been?" Ms. Spencer says, "Well some situations has improved, but then I got into another situation that's very hard for me to deal with." Bruce says, "Sounds like you jumped out of the frying pan into the fire." Ms. Spencer says, "You are about right." Bruce asks, "What is it, you know you can tell me anything. We've been friends forever." Ms. Spencer says, "I need you to do me a favor. It's about a relationship that I need to break off. All I need you to do is to come over this evening and play as though you are my lover." Bruce tells her that he doesn't want to get in any kind of trouble. Ms. Spencer assures him that he wouldn't. She told him that she wants him to come over about 4:00 pm, the time she knew James would be off from work. Bruce tells her that he would do it.

Later that day Bruce drives up and rings the door bell. Ms. Spencer opens the door and rushes Bruce in the house. So she set the stage for her son to be in his room playing video games. Then she told Bruce to come with her in her room. Bruce just took his shirt and shoes off. Ms. Spencer had on a gown and they both got into bed.

Soon or later James drives up and he notices that a car was there that he had not seen before. James looks at the car thinking it may be a relative of hers. So he walks on up to the front door and enters his key. When he got in the house he took his coat off and laid it on the chair and loosens his tie around his neck. Then he turns around and sees his luggage by the door. He calls for Ms. Spencer but she doesn't answer. So he looks in the kitchen and he didn't see her there. Ms. Spencer tells Bruce to act as though they were making love. James opens the bedroom door and sees Bruce in the bed with her. James yells, "Betty, what are you doing?!" Betty just pulls the sheet up over her chest acting as though she was surprised. Bruce continues to lay there looking at James. James puts his hands over his face and falls down on his knees at the foot of the bed and saying, "Betty no, Betty no!" Then he jumps up and storms out of the room full of anger and confusion, grabs his coat off the chair, picks his luggage up and storms out of the door.

Ms. Spencer began to cry and Bruce consoles her. Crying, she tells Bruce that she love James so much. If she didn't let him go now, it would have been impossible. She told him that James was a good man. Bruce says, "I got an idea why you did it, he's married and you don't want to be the cause of him leaving his wife." Crying, Ms. Spencer says, "It hurts so much but I had to do it." Consoling her Bruce says, "I know."

James had checked into a motel on the second floor. With just his pants on, James is drinking a bottle of liquor trying to ease his mind. He drinks so much until he passes out on the bed. When he wakes up the next morning, he looks at his watch and sees that it's passed the time that he is to be at work. So he hurries and reaches on the night stand to get his cell phone to call the School. He tells them that he won't be in because he wasn't feeling well. Then he goes to the bathroom and puts cold water on his face. As he dries his face, he looks in the mirror at himself, covers his face with the towel and says, "Oh my God!" James storms out of the bathroom and grabs the bottle of liquor. This time he uses a glass and keeps pouring and pouring one drink after another. James is in emotional distress because he not only has lost Ms. Spencer, but he's too ashamed to go back home to his wife.

Later that evening, James is walking in the lower parts of town feeling numb. Out of all the drinking he had done, it seems as though he couldn't get rid of the pain of what a mess he has made of his life. So it happens that a drug dealer was watching him as he passes by and says, "My Man, I got that thing." James turns around with the expression like, are you talking to me? The drug dealer says, "Yea, I am talking to you. You look like you need a little boost and I got just the thing that you need." James walks up a little closer to the guy. James says, "You maybe on target, my friend, what you got?" The guy tells him to follow him. James goes with the guy and he goes on the side of the building where there's not much light. The guy reaches in his pocket and pulls out a plastic bag with packages of coke, marijuana and crack cocaine in it. James knew what each one of them was, so James decides to take a couple of packs of coke. Then James asked the guy how much he owed him. The guy told him that he doesn't fool with nickel and dime stuff, all his stuff is twenty-five dollars apiece. James pulls out his wallet and gives the guy a fifty dollar bill. The guy takes the money and looks at James and says, "Yea my Man, you must be new at this pulling your wallet out like that showing all that cash on you. Let me give you some advice. You got some thugs will sell to you and have somebody to rob you Man. But I am cool.

The next time you buy from somebody, show just enough money for what you're paying for. You dig?" James stretches his eyes and tells the guy thanks. The guy says, "You know where to find me that's my spot but I don't be out here during the day time, my cut buddy works for me doing the day, Ok? See you Blood." James shakes his hand like he's in church and the guy laughs and says, "Man this is how we shake hands on the street. He shows James and they laugh then James walks away.

The same night Gucci and Marsha are at Big Momma's house in separate rooms. Gucci is in the room next to Marsha with a Hispanic man. While the Hispanic man is in the bathroom, Gucci hurries and calls the cab driver on his cell phone, then he takes the man wallet out of his pants and eases out of the room. Then Gucci hurries and knocks on the door where Marsha is. Marsha opens the door. Gucci whispers and tells Marsha that he's leaving and he'll meet her back at the apartment. The Hispanic man comes out of the bathroom and sees that Gucci has left. He immediately checks his pants pocket on the bed.

When he finds that his wallet was gone, he hurried and got dressed and went to the desk counter to Big Momma and told her what just happened. Big Momma says, "Well what do you want me to do, I just rent rooms. That was your date that you picked up and brought here." The Hispanic man said, "That's alright when I catch up with her, I am going show her what we do to people like her in my Country." Then he storms out of the door very angry.

Gucci is at home taking off his makeup. Marsha walks in the house, places her purse on the table and calls out for Gucci. Gucci says, "Hey girl, I am in my room." Marsha goes to Gucci's room and says, "Gucci what was that all about, I know you didn't do what I think you did." Gucci laughs and says, "Girl, he was loaded." Marsha excited asks, "How much Gucci?" Gucci says, "Over two thousand dollars girl in one hundred dollar bills. We hit it big!" Marsha says, "Let me see!" Gucci takes the money out of the man's wallet and spreads it across the bed. Marsha jumps on the bed and picks up the money and says, "We are rich!"

It's about noon time and Brenda is in the living room going over the mail. As she opens the letter from her credit card statement, she notices the charges that were from a motel and large amounts of cash withdrawals. It was charges that James had made since he left from Ms. Spencer's house. She began to think of where the charges were made. So she looks again at the name of the motel where the charges were made. She knew it had to be James because she didn't use the card for a motel. So she waited until later that evening to call James on his cell phone. James was in his motel room drinking and snorting cocaine. James answers his phone. Brenda says, "Hello James this is Brenda.

James freezes and then he tries to collect himself. Brenda says, "James, are you there?" James says, "Yea I am here." Brenda asks, "Where are you?" James says, "I am at a motel." Brenda asks him how long has he been there. James tells her about a month and a half. Brenda tells him that she called because she saw the charges on the bill statement. Brenda asks him why he didn't come home. He told her that he was messed up. Brenda asks him what does he mean by he was messed up. James tells her that he don't want to talk about it right now. Brenda breaks down and cries and tells James that she loves him, and to come home they could work things out. James takes the phone from his ear and holds it awhile in his hand, drops his head down because he couldn't stand to hear Brenda crying.

James hangs up the phone and falls down on his knees crying asking God to help him. James had gotten to a point that he knew he needed God's help because he realized that he couldn't help himself.

The next day Brenda goes over her mother-in-law, (Mrs. Gibson) house and tells her that she had found out where James was. Mrs. Gibson asks Brenda why James went to a motel when he could have come home or to her house. She tells Brenda that James ought to know that we'll forgive him if he wanted to come back home. Brenda sadly says, "I know Momma, but he said something about he was in a mess. I tried to find out what he was talking about but before I knew it he had hung up the phone." Mrs. Gibson says, "Probably things didn't work out between him and that other woman and he's too ashamed to face either one of us. At least I hope that it's all that he's messed up about. But James knows that I didn't raise him up like that!" Then Mrs. Gibson began to cry saying, "I hope he's alright."

James is in his office at school. The secretary comes in and welcomes him back. James tells her that he doesn't know how long he's going to be back because he's not out of the woods yet. The secretary asks him did he have the flu or something. James tells her he doesn't know what it was but it left him kind of weak. James knew what was wrong with him and what he had been doing. The secretary tells James that he may have returned back to work too early and needed more time to heal. James tells her that he was thinking about asking the principle for a leave of absents. The secretary tells James that the last time she checked he had about three months of vacation time. She tells him that he knows he hardly ever takes time off and he has plenty of sick time.

She tells him if he wants her to put the request in she would. She said, "Everybody needs a little time off some time. James asks, "Would you do that for me?" She said, "No problem, when do you want me to date it for?" James tells her starting tomorrow for about three months. She tells James that she will type up the request for him and bring it to him to sign. James tells her thanks, she's life saver. After the secretary leaves, James starts to think about how he's started lying and puts his hands over his face and shakes his head.

Later that evening Brenda gets in her car and starts looking for the motel where James is staying. When she got there, she parks her car, gets out and goes in up to the front desk and asks the clerk for the room number for Mr. James Gibson. The clerk looks up James's name in the system and tells her the room number. Brenda tells her thanks and walks up the stairs to his room. Brenda knocks on the door. James is at the table snorting and drinking. He hears the knock on the door. James gets up and goes to the door and peeps through the peep hole and sees that it's Brenda. So he immediately rushes to clear and hide everything. Then James opens the door. Brenda comes in and hugs him. James holds her in his arms and says, "Baby I am so sorry." Brenda says, "It's alright, I know how you feel."

James tells her to have a seat, and they both sit down on the sofa. Brenda asks James how he has been. James tells her not too well. Brenda tells him that the children miss him. James tells her he misses them too. Then he gets up and starts to walk around and says to Brenda, "You shouldn't have come." Brenda says, "I am still your wife I love you. What did you expect me to do after I found out where you were, just wait at the house hoping you would come home?" James is becoming irritated because he felt like he needed a drink but he didn't want Brenda to know the habits that he had picked up.

So he picks an argument with Brenda hoping that she would get angry and leave. James says to her, "I am glad to see you Brenda but I am expecting someone." Brenda asks him, "who?" James says, "I've been seeing another woman and she's going to be here any moment." Just as he expected, Brenda jumps up and says, "Maybe we can talk another time." James says, "Sure," and Brenda leaves. James starts acting like a real addict looking for his drink and cocaine. After he gets it he hurries and sits at the table, shaking as he opens the bottle and drinks straight out of the bottle. Then he snorts some cocaine and feels himself calming down.

Later that night Gucci and Marsha are at a club sitting at their table. This time they're dressed in their normal attire. Gucci is dressed in men clothing and Marsha is dressed in normal attire without the flashy wigs on. While they're sitting at their table with drinks, the Spanish guy that Gucci stole the money from walks in the door and goes up to the counter to order a drink. Gucci spots him. Gucci's eyes stretched real big and he put his hand over his mouth. Marsha looks at him and says, "Gucci, what's wrong, who do you see?" Gucci says, "That's him." Marsha says, "Him who?" Gucci whispers and says, "The man I robbed!" Marsha says, "Oh my goodness, what are we going to do?!" Gucci says, "I just hope he doesn't look this way!" Marsha says, "Oh don't worry he won't recognize you." Gucci says, "What do you mean?" Marsha says, "Gucci you're dressed like a man." Gucci thinks and says, "Oh girl I forgot" and they both started laughing. Sure enough the man looked around and didn't recognize him. So they just played it off and continued drinking and talking and the man eventually left.

The next day Brenda is at her mother-in-law's house telling her about James and how different he has become. Her mother-in-law says, "Don't pay that any attention, he's probably trying to discourage you from coming over there because he knows he's doing something wrong." Brenda says, "You know you may be right because it seems like I smelled some liquor on his breath. I didn't want to believe it at the time because I was so glad to see him. I didn't want to question him. It really slipped my mind when he told me that he was expecting someone over. So I took it as though he wanted me to leave." Her mother-in-law says, "Brenda you stick with him, don't stop going over there and soon or later you'll catch up with what he's doing. I am surprised that he hasn't called me. So you know definitely he's into something he doesn't know anything about. He's good and ashamed because he knows that he was taught better. Whatever it is, it's about to get the best of him and Brenda we have to pray. It's nothing too hard for God. You get with your children one night and tell them we got to pray for Daddy." They console each other and her mother-in-law begins to cry out to the Lord saying, "Lord this is my son that I raised to honor you Lord and has gone astray. Help us Lord bringing him back to his senses. Bring him back Lord to his wife and children. Most of all bring him back to you Lord. In Jesus name I pray, amen."

That night James goes in to town to draw some money out of the ATM machine. Then he goes straight to the dope dealer's corner to buy some drugs. But this time the drug dealer introduces crack cocaine to him. He tells James that he's fresh out of powder, but that was to get James started on it to make him really hooked. James says, "I don't know man that might be a little too much for me." The dealer says, "Try it man you might like it. It's a better rush. But don't drink that hard stuff like liquor, maybe a little wine or a beer." James says, "Ok I'll try it, how much is it?" The dealer says, "Twenty five cents apiece." James says, "Give me four." James pulls out his wallet and gives the dealer a hundred dollar bill. The dealer says, "Man didn't I tell you not to pull your wallet out like that? Because sometimes these thugs sell you something and rob you at the same time." James says, "Sorry man I forgot." The dealer says, Yea man now you got to buy you a pipe to smoke that with." James asked, "A pipe, what do you mean?" The dealer says, "Hey look man I am going to do you a favor since you're one of my best customers. I'll ride with you to the shop and we'll pick up what you need to smoke it with and take you to my crib to show you how to do it." James says, "That's a bet."

Later that night Brenda is home with the kids getting them ready for bed. Afterward she tells them that they are going to pray for daddy. Her son asks, "Why mommy, is daddy sick? When is daddy coming home?" Brenda tells him, "We are going to put it in the hands of the Lord, that's why we need to pray." Then her son says, "The Lord will do it won't he mom?" Brenda says, "Yes He will." Then her son says, "I believe it mom." Brenda almost breaks down in tears but she tries to hold them back and says, "Come on you guys let's get on our knees and pray." The kids kneel down beside her by the bed and she tells them to repeat after her. Brenda begins by saying, "Lord this is our prayer for daddy. Please hear us Lord, bring daddy back home safe from harm and danger. Let your grace and mercy abound and find a way as we humbly bow down to thee, amen." Then Brenda puts her son to bed, kisses him and says goodnight. Then she grabs her daughter by the hand and takes her to her room and puts her to bed.

The next day Brenda gets a letter from the mortgage company stating that their mortgage is two months behind. Brenda is appalled. She didn't know that James was not paying the mortgage. She calls James on his cell phone. James is asleep in his bed. He rolls over and answers his cell phone. Brenda says, "Hi James, are you busy?" James says, "No I was asleep." Brenda says, "Asleep, where are you?" James catches himself and goes in complete silence because he forgot that he hadn't told Brenda that he had taken off from work. Brenda says, "James, are you still there? Where are you?" James says, "I am at the motel."

Brenda says, "Why, are sick or something?" I thought you were at work." James says, "No I took some time off to get myself together. I have paid leave of absence." Brenda says, "I called you because we got a letter in the mail stating that the mortgage is two months behind. Now what is going on? You always paid the bills on time. Does that lady have you so messed up that you can't work and think of the kids not having a roof over their head? What are you doing with your money? I hope that you just forgot to pay the mortgage and haven't spent the money." James rubs his head and says, "Baby please don't be angry, I'll straighten out everything." Brenda says, "No all of this doesn't sound right, I am coming over there!" James says, "I told you that I was going to handle everything. Just hold on." Brenda hangs up the phone.

Brenda gets up and rushes to the bedroom to get her purse and leaves to go where James is staying. James is sitting on the bed and he reaches on the night stand to get his pipe and cocaine and starts smoking and then he goes to the kitchen to get a wine cooler. He goes back to his room and began to smoke and drink very frustrated.

About two hours later Brenda knocks on the door. James hears the knock at the door. He's begins to tremble trying to get himself together. Brenda knocks again. James gets up and stumbles his way to the door. He opens the door still in his underwear looking wild in the face. Brenda looks at him and says, "James what in the world have you been doing!? Look at you, you're a mess!" James says, "Brenda comes in so I can shut the door." Brenda goes in and starts looking around. There are plates with leftover food in them in the living room and empty bottles of wine coolers everywhere. Brenda says, "James you're living like a pig! When did you start doing all this?"

Then she heads to his bedroom and looks at his bed and the night stand. She sees the wine coolers and cocaine pipe. She flops on the bed and grabs her face and says, "Oh no, this couldn't be happening." James comes to the bedroom door and sees Brenda sitting there crying. James goes and sits down by her and says, "Baby I am sorry, I am messed up, and I didn't want you to see me like this. I can't help myself, I feel so bad." Brenda looks at him and realizes that he doesn't need any more pressure than what he has so she consoles him and says, "James we're going to get through this with the Lord's help. I know this is not you." While she is holding him in her arms James began to relax and nods off a little bit. Brenda tells him to wake up and lay down in the bed. She puts the cover over him like a baby and kisses him on the forehead. James goes sound asleep. She stands there looking at him sleep. Realizing that he's on drugs, she takes his wallet out of his pants pockets. As she looks through his wallet, she notices that he has a lot of cash. So Brenda leaves the cash and takes the credit cards and his bank card. Then she turns around and looks at James in the bed sleeping, and then she leaves.

The next day Brenda goes over to James's mother house. Brenda and her mother-in-law are sitting in the living room talking about James. Brenda says, "Momma I hate to tell you this but James is on drugs. I went over to his apartment yesterday because I had received a letter from the mortgage company that we were two months behind in payments. I thought he was paying the mortgage he always paid the bills. I never had to worry about anything not being paid. So I took the credit cards and bank card out of his wallet before I left so the bills can be paid. His school check is direct deposited. I hope that he hasn't drained his account because he sure had a lot of cash in his wallet." Mrs. Gibson says, oh no Baby, you mean to tell me James done got that bad! How did you find out that he was on drugs?" Brenda says, "Momma when I got there and saw the way he looked and the conditions of his apartment with wine coolers and beer cans all over the place, I went to his room and that's when I saw the drugs." Mrs. Gibson drops her head and began to cry saying, "Oh Lord help him. This is not my child. You know how I raised him and how he loved working in the church. Please Lord, help him." Brenda rubs her on the back and says, "Momma, don't cry. We just have to pray."

Later that night James is walking going to buy some more drugs. This time there's two new guys selling drugs in the spot where James usually goes. James spots them and walks up to them and asks where Earnest was. One of the guys answered and said, "We handling this spot tonight. What do you want? We got the same thing." James was kind of hesitant at first, and then James says, "Give me four rocks and a bag of weed." The two guys look at each other and laughs. James says, Man, what's so funny?" One of them says, "Man you don't expect us to just pull everything out on the front like this, follow us." The two guys start walking on the side of the building. James follows them. Then they stop and start beating James. One takes James's wallet and they both take off leaving James on the ground. James lays there for a while and finally makes his way up on his feet. He stumbles out of the alley with his face all blooded up. He makes it to his car and drives away.

When James gets home he tries to clean himself up in the bathroom. Now he has no ID, his driver's license is missing and his face is swollen. Good thing Brenda took his credit cards and bank card out of his wallet before she left. Then James realizes that he doesn't have any dope, so he opens a bottle of liquor and takes drinks after drink until he passes out.

The next evening Marsha gets dropped off by the cab driver at Gucci's apartment. She walks to the front door and searches for her keys in her purse. Then as she starts to stick the key in the door, she notices that the door was slightly cracked open. So she eases the door open and slowly walks in the house looking around and began to call out to Gucci. She looks in the kitchen and then Gucci's bedroom. There still dressed in drag clothes Gucci is laying across the bed face up with his throat slashed and one of his hands cut off. Marsha screams hysterically and runs out of the room crying. She grabs her purse and storms out of the house. She runs as fast as she can towards the street. When she reaches the main street where there's lighting, she notices a phone booth nearby. So she runs to the phone booth just to hide, and stoop down so no one can see her, and uses her cell phone to call Eunice. Eunice is in her bedroom on the computer. Eunice cell phone rings. Eunice picks her cell phone up that's on her computer desktop. Eunice answers and says, "Hello." Marsha crying says, "Eunice this me, Marsha, please come get me!" Eunice says, "Come get you, what do you mean come get you, what's wrong?" Marsha says, "Somebody just killed Gucci. Please hurry I am so scared!" Eunice says, "Oh my God, where are you!?" Marsha says, I am on Hill lane and 46th Street in front of Jerry's grocery store in the phone booth, please hurry Eunice please!" Eunice says, "I think I know where that is. I am coming now." Eunice hangs up the phone, grabs her purse. As she grabs her purse her phone rings again. Eunice sits on her bed and answers her phone.

Eunice says, "Hello". James is shaking because he needs a fix. James says, "Hey Baby girl this is Bro I need you to do me a big favor it's very important." Eunice says, "James is this you! Momma has been so worried about you! How are you doing?" James says, "Not to good Sis, I got robbed and my wallet and everything is gone." Eunice says, "Oh my God, what is going on with everybody?!" James says, "Don't worry about it I need you to come and bring me a hundred dollars as soon as you can! Please Sis, I really need it bad!" Eunice asks, "Where are you staying? Hold on let me get a pen and paper." Eunice gets a pen and a sheet of paper off the desk of her computer. Eunice says, "Ok give me the address." James says, "The name of the motel is Shannon right off the highway called Straight Street on 72nd and Muriel Ave, you can't miss it. It's a white building and I am on the 2nd floor room 211. Are you coming?" Eunice says, "Yes I'll be there as soon as I can." Eunice rushes out of the room and peeps in her mother's room and sees that she is sleeping. Then she rushes out of the house and gets in her car and leaves.

James calls Earnest, his regular dope man, and tells him what had happen and he needs him to come to his house to bring him some dope. By the time he hangs up the phone, Brenda knocks on the door. James rushes to the door because he thinks its Eunice bringing him some money. James opens the door and Brenda looks at him and says, "James, you look a mess, what's happening to you!?" James hands starts shaking with his eyes stretched wide as though he didn't know who Brenda was. Brenda comes in and says, "James are you high, this is Brenda." Still shaking James says, "Yea I know who you are it's just that I thought you were somebody else. Have a seat. Did you bring any money with you? I need some bad Baby, I hope you say yes, please Baby say yes." Brenda says, "James hold on a minute, just calm down, money for what? I not so long ago left here and I checked your wallet and you had hundreds of dollars in there. It's only been what one or two days? And no all I have is about twenty dollars in my purse."

Then there's another knock at the door. It's Earnest the dope dealer. James opens the door and says, "Hey Man, come on in. Did you bring that with you?" Earnest walks in and he asks, "Who's this pretty little thing?" James says, that my wife Brenda, Brenda this is Earnest a friend of mine. Brenda looking puzzled says, "Hi nice to meet you." James tells Brenda to excuse them a little while he'll be right back. He and Earnest goes in James's room. James asks, "Man what you got?" Earnest says, "Baby Boy I got whatever you need." They both start laughing. James says, Man I don't have any money right now; you know I told you what happened. But my sister is on her way right now to bring me some money." Earnest says, "I don't know about that Man, this is other folk dope and they don't play." James starts shaking and says, "Man come on you know I am good for it." Earnest says, "I might pay it for you if you give me a taste of your sweet honey out there." James says, "No Man, come on, you got to be joking." Earnest looks at James real seriously and says, "Do I look like I am joking? Go out there and talk to her. That if you need it that bad, it's up to you or I got to go." James says, "No Man, don't do this to me, please."

Earnest says, "Man let me get out of here." James desperate, says, "Wait let me see." James goes in the living room where Brenda is sitting on the sofa. He walks up to her looking crazy. He sits down by Brenda on the sofa and says, Brenda I am sick and Earnest is going to give me some medicine. Just go in there with him for a while. He just wants you to talk to him while I take the medicine. Please Baby do it for me just go in there and sit on the bed and talk to him." Brenda says, "James you must be out of your mind." James knew he was lying but he was desperate. Then he began to cry in Brenda's lap. Brenda just looks down at him with tears in her eyes and says, "If you don't think any more of me than that, this draws the line James." Then she gets up and walks to the room. James walks behind her and tells Earnest to step out of the room and James shuts the door behind him. Earnest smiles and says, "That's my boy now what you want?" James says, yea four rocks." Earnest reaches in his pocket and gets the plastic bags of rocks out. Earnest gives him four big ones. James smiles and says, "Man these looks nice. Just go on in the room and but first hand me my pipe off the dresser." Earnest goes in the room gets the pipe off the dresser and cracks the door and hand it to James.

James immediately goes and sits down at the kitchen table, puts some dope in his pipe and began to smoke very deeply. He begins to relax. Then he smokes, and smokes. He gets more relaxed. Then he hears Brenda scream and he catches himself. He looks at the drugs as though he hated what he has become and knocks over the table. He puts his hands over his face saying, "Oh no, oh no!" He storms out of the kitchen to his room like a mad man and kicks in the door. He sees Earnest and Brenda in the bed fully clothed and Brenda trying to fight Earnest off of her.

Eunice and Marsha are coming up the stairs outside on their way to James apartment. James is in the room beating Earnest. Brenda sits up on the bed watching James beat Earnest. James has Earnest on the floor steady punching him. Earnest is bleeding out of the mouth badly. Brenda yells out, "James that's enough you're killing him!" James gets off of him and storms out of the room. Brenda gets up off the bed and runs behind James. Eunice and Marsha is standing at the door getting ready to knock and James storms out of the door Brenda right behind him almost to knock both Eunice and Marsha down and heads down the stairs. Eunice and Marsha take off behind them down the stairs trying to see what was going on. When James gets outside, he takes off down the street with Brenda right behind him.

Marsha and Eunice are running behind Brenda trying to catch up. They are all running behind James down the street. Brenda is running behind James barely able to keep up with him. Eunice and Marsha are behind Brenda trying to keep up with both of them. James spots a church and starts running towards it. The church had two large glass designs with the picture of Jesus that fitted all the way down to the edge of the block on the ground with big wide doors in between. James ran up to the church glass design and busted straight through to inside the church. His hands and face is bloody. James falls to the floor and start crawling down the aisle crying saying, "Lord help me!" There was a huge cross behind the pulpit in view. James kept crawling towards the cross saying, "Lord help me!" By that time

Brenda, Eunice and Marsha had made it there and they saw the glass was broken out and they carefully stepped in the church and saw James crawling down the aisle looking up at the cross. All of a sudden I was told that the cross began to give off a sun like glare that lit up the hold church and a cool breeze started blowing from the cross. Brenda, Marsha, and Eunice saw it and fell to their knees behind James. They all had tears falling from their faces staring at the cross.

About two weeks later on a Sunday, the pastor is up speaking getting ready to introduce James. The pastor says, "I would like to give honor to God my loving Savior Jesus Christ and to the Elders, Ministers of the gospel, to the deacons, mothers and to the congregation. I count it a blessing to be before you on this wonderful day. I would like to introduce to you a man that all of you know, that has great abilities, a man that has been returned to us by the mighty hands of God. God is a forgiving God and He said in His word that we must forgive in order for Him to forgive us. Isn't that right saints?" The congregation says, "Amen." "He's like a son to me. Maybe I'll even call him the prodigal son. His name is Minister James Gibson, husband of Mrs. Brenda Gibson and son of Mother Gibson. But before he comes the choir is going to give us a beautiful selection. Let everybody say amen." The congregation says, "Amen."

After the choir sings, James gets his bible and walks up to the roster, shakes the pastor's hand and stands before the congregation. Then he says, "Giving honor to my Lord and Savior Jesus Christ, whom I wouldn't be here if it wasn't for Him. I give honor to everyone in their respectful places." Then he pauses and looks in the congregation at his wife and kids, Marsha and her family, and then he looks up to God and looks over the congregation and says, "The title of my sermon today is, "*Snatched from the Fire.*"

Printed in the United States
By Bookmasters